BOLLYWOOD
2
ACADEMY
Melody
Queen
PUNEET BHANDAL

First published in the United Kingdom in 2023 by Lantana Publishing Ltd.
Clavier House, 21 Fifth Road, Newbury RG14 6DN, UK
www.lantanapublishing.com | info@lantanapublishing.com

American edition published in 2023 by Lantana Publishing Ltd., UK.

Cover and internal illustrations by Jen Khatun.

Distributed in the United States and Canada by Lerner Publishing Group, Inc.
241 First Avenue North, Minneapolis, MN 55401 U.S.A.
For reading levels and more, look for this title at www.lernerbooks.com
Cataloging-in-Publication Data Available.

Hardcover ISBN: 978-1-915244-28-4
ePDF ISBN: 978-1-915244-29-1
ePub3 S&L ISBN: 978-1-915244-30-7
ePub3 Trade ISBN: 978-1-915244-31-4

Printed and bound in China using plant-based inks on sustainably sourced paper.

For Mili.

Your sparkly, kind and unique personality was the inspiration for this book.

GAMES ROOM
Jai
DaD
Mum
zeesHaN
Wish you were here!
music studio
NOISE ZONE
MR Pereira
Miss Takkar
DJ DAN
om.om
PEACE
om.om
Gauri
'The BEST'

MELODY QUEEN

By Puneet Bhandal

music studio
NOISE
ZONE

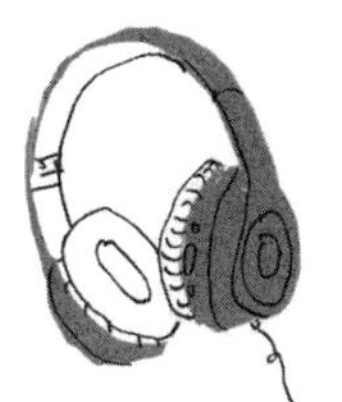

TAKE ONE

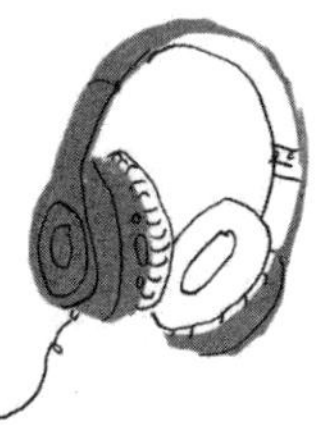

My eyes danced as I watched Zeeshan, my best friend at the Bollywood Academy, strum a tune he'd composed. His curly hair flopped rhythmically over his face as he plucked the strings of his guitar. When he'd finished, he patted the guitar affectionately before putting it down.

"That was awesome, Zee!" I exclaimed, clapping loudly. "Especially the chorus."

A Zoom call wasn't the easiest way for our band, B-Tunes, to share music, but during the summer vacation it was the only way.

"By the time we get back to school, I'll pen some wicked lyrics to go with that," said Raktim from the vast living room of his home in Nepal.

"And I can't wait to add vocals," smiled Joya, the lead singer and final member of our quartet.

"Thanks, guys!" said Zeeshan, looking flattered. "But right now, I gotta go. Let me know if we can squeeze in another session before school starts. I'll call you later, Sim. I need you to fix the piano part for my new song."

"Sure," I smiled. Knowing what a great musician Zeeshan was, I felt proud when he asked me for

advice. Music had bonded us from our first days at the Bollywood Academy. "Over and out," he waved, then disappeared from the screen.

"I'm off too," said Raktim, flashing a big, happy smile and radiating his usual positive energy. "See you both soon. If not online, then in real life next week!"

"See ya, Simi," said Joya once Raktim had also vanished. "I'm off to do my final bits of shopping for the new semester. I'm so glad we get to share a room again!" she added. "See you next week!"

I snapped my laptop shut, excited to think we'd all be back together in a matter of days to start Grade 7.

"Simi!"

I sighed. "Coming, Mom!" I called before running downstairs. "I was just on a call with B-Tunes."

"Always music, music, music!" moaned Mom, looking particularly glamorous in a red chiffon saree with a mirrorwork blouse that glistened as she turned. The sunlight streaming in through the window was bouncing off her, making her sparkle like a disco ball. "For somebody who's going to be a Bollywood actress, there are better things you could be doing."

"Like playing a piano in our music room?" I said sassily. She knew I wanted my own piano so badly, and I knew she'd never get me one.

"Uff, not that again!" Mom folded her arms in annoyance. "It's a living room, not a music room," she reminded me.

I spooned some Bombay Mix out of a jar and munched on it.

"The Bollywood Academy isn't cheap, you know?" Mom glared at me when I didn't reply. "You're too laidback," she went on, admiring the red nails and white tips of her brand new manicure. "And you spend too much time doing silly things on that music app when you should be learning how to emote and—"

"Mom," I cut in, "I've heard this speech before. There's only so much acting practice I can do. All kids have hobbies. Careers are for adults."

"Very smart!" she kicked in. "You also need to get good grades to keep your place at school. I hope you finished all your homework? There are just a few days before you go back."

I decided to move the conversation in a new direction.

"You look nice, Mom," I said, slipping my phone into my pocket before she could mention my music app again.

"Do I?" She turned to look at me, her sharp features softening instantly. It always worked. "I'm off to an audition – to be on the judging panel of a new game

show on Starshine TV," she told me.

"Hugratulations, Mom!" I replied, giving her a congratulatory hug. It was something I always said if somebody shared good news with me. "That's great!"

And of course it was amazing to get a big opening like that. Except...I knew the chance of Mom scoring the job was pretty slim. She was always outdone by someone younger, more famous, or with better connections. Being married to Shyam Prasad – my dad and one of the biggest movie stars in the South Indian state of Telangana – was perhaps the only reason Mom got auditions in the first place. Before I was born, she had been much less successful at getting movie roles than Dad had been. It was even more difficult for her now, while Dad was still in constant demand.

Poor Mom.

I gave her a peck on the cheek as she grabbed her glitzy handbag and teetered off. She quickly glanced at the side of her face in the big gold-leaf mirror before she stepped out – making sure I hadn't dented her makeup with my kiss, no doubt.

"Gauri's making dinner and your dad will be home 9ish," she shouted as she got into the back seat of our Bentley where our driver, Rajiv, was waiting. "Oh, and I told your auntie that you would Facetime Priya today.

You haven't spoken to her in such a long time. Make sure you do it."

Luckily, she didn't wait for a reply. There was no way I was going to call Perfect Priya if I could avoid it. There was nothing wrong with my cousin – in fact, it was the opposite. She was the one person who could do no wrong, while I was always getting into trouble.

I waved as the gray car rolled out of sight.

"Your food's ready – eat," said Gauri, tying the loose end of her saree tightly around her waist.

I reflected that I'd probably spent more hours of my life with our housekeeper than with my own mother. Considering Mom didn't have a job as such, this struck me as a little ironic, but maintaining herself to the standard she did with all those hair and skincare appointments was like a job in itself.

On the plus side, Gauri let me get away with so much. "Off to the studio again," I smirked as I ran back upstairs to rehearse some more.

Even though I didn't have a piano yet, I adored my studio. It was basic – a computer with Digital Audio Workstation software, an electronic keyboard, headphones, speakers and mics – but I was adding to it all the time. My birthday and Christmas wish lists always featured musical items.

I switched on my Mac, put my headphones on, and selected a piece of music I'd made earlier in the week. I set about changing the arrangement. It was too repetitive and needed remixing. For me, there was nothing more satisfying than creating new melodies on my keyboard or listening to tracks and trying to work out which two to put together to make a great mix.

I was proud that I was self-taught. I would gladly have had musical tuition if it had been offered to me but I'd been pushed toward dance classes and youth theatre all my life given that I was going to become an actor.

"Uff, you scared me!"

I jumped when Gauri prodded me. She was saying something but I couldn't hear her. I removed my headphones.

"I've been shouting for you," she told me. "The boys are downstairs."

I glanced up at the clock. "Sheesh!" I'd completely forgotten about cricket practice. I shoved on my sneakers and rushed downstairs.

"Sorry for making you wait, boys," I said, catching my breath.

"Where's the Bentley?" asked 5-year-old Viraj. He was the little brother of my childhood bestie, Jai.

"Mom's taken it to an audition, but I promise you can

ride in it soon."

"We want a ride too!" said Roshan, another neighborhood kid.

"You'll all get a turn," I told them, smiling.

"Here," Jai said, handing me a cricket magazine.

"Oh, wow!" I exclaimed, glancing at the cover which featured my favorite bowler, Suresh. "You're the best, Jai! You're the only one who gets me these!" I hugged him tight.

Jai and I were the same age and had been friends since the age of four. I grabbed his cheeks. "*Soooo cute!*" I laughed. It was something all the aunties did to him when he was young as he'd had the plumpest cheeks.

"Are we gonna do this for ever, Sim?"

"You bet!" I chuckled as we made tracks for the tree-lined road that led to the Jubilee Hills Cricket Club.

It was a beautiful day in Film Nagar, the chic neighborhood in Hyderabad where we lived. And it wasn't as sticky and hot as it had been at the start of the summer break.

"I wish you were all at the Bollywood Academy," I said as we strolled past a row of designer shops. "I'm gonna miss playing with you guys when I go back." The boys laughed as I told them how my team hadn't even made thirty runs in the last cricket tournament at school.

"It's weird when you're not around," admitted Jai. "We go back to being an all-boys' club. No other girls around here are interested in playing."

I was lucky for sure. Jubilee Hills Cricket Club didn't treat me any differently because I was a girl. They'd always welcomed and accepted me – much to my mom's annoyance.

We arrived at the club to find Govind, the manager, checking the stumps of the wicket in preparation. He looked sharp in his all white uniform.

"How's your superstar dad?" he asked, looking up as we approached.

"Good, thank you," I replied.

"Remind him about the party this weekend," he added as we got ready to start the game.

"What party, uncle?"

"It's Mohan's 60th birthday. Actually, don't worry, I'll remind Shyam myself later on," he muttered as I took up my position. I was batting first.

It was just as well Govind had taken it upon himself to let Dad know. I'd forgotten all about the party by the time I left the club. True to his word, Govind was on the phone to Dad when I got home.

"I suppose I should go," said Dad, stroking his salt and pepper moustache. Dad's hair was graying but he still looked pretty young for a 45-year-old – it was a good job too as he was still playing characters at least a decade younger than his age. "I haven't seen Mohan for a while. Who else is coming?"

I gave Dad a hug before taking off my hat and untying my shoelaces.

"DJ Dan?" Dad said to Govind. "Who's DJ Dan?"

"*What!*" I shouted out. "Did you say DJ Dan?"

Dad moved the handset away from his ear. "Some DJ at a party this weekend. You know who he is?"

"Oh. My. Goodness!" I yelled. "*The* most famous DJ and YouTuber in the whole of India, Dad! How do you not know? Can we go?"

It must have been the sight of me jumping up and down that made him chuckle. "Okay, Govind, done! We'll be there."

"Yes!" I went and squeezed Dad tight. I was so excited. "I have to call Zeeshan and tell him about this!" Zeeshan was an even bigger Dan fan than me – he was hooked on his YouTube channel and had his T-shirts and everything.

"Put Radhika's name down too," Dad told Govind as I darted up the stairs to get my phone. "We'll be there at 8pm sharp."

TAKE TWO

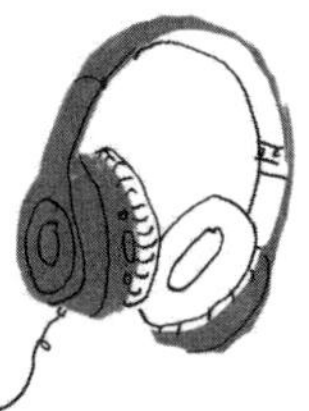

Dad was a stickler for punctuality. At exactly 8pm on Saturday, we pulled up outside one of the many mansions in the exclusive Banjara Hills area of Film Nagar. True to its name, Film Nagar was home to the Telugu language film industry. Countless studios and production houses were located there.

Mom straightened out her outfit – a smart pant suit with an intricately-embroidered jacket worn over the top – and smoothed down her hair as we made our way to the entrance.

"You know what I think of casual clothes at formal functions, don't you, Simi?" Mom said pointedly as she spotted a small group of photographers outside the house. Their cameras were facing in our direction.

I shrugged my shoulders. Mom had been so busy getting herself ready, she hadn't had a chance to pester me to change. That suited me fine. She would have no doubt made me wear a party dress and I hated them. Jumpsuits were perfect for impromptu games of soccer or doing cartwheels when bored.

"Dress like a lady when you go to events," she

scolded as quietly as she could. "Priya always dresses immaculately, and she's a year younger than you."

Would Mom ever stop comparing me to her?

"You never know who's going to take your photo and where it will appear," she went on, running her fingers through my thick, wavy hair to tidy it up.

"Sim looks fine to me. It's a perfectly stylish choice," Dad stated as I scoured the parking lot looking for DJ Dan.

I still couldn't believe such a big YouTuber would be performing at a house party. I'd subscribed to DJ Dan's YouTube channel when I was eight and had learned so much about music through his tutorials. This year, his popularity had gone through the roof after releasing some Bollywood remixes that had gone viral. I loved that he was now mainstream, but his recent fame meant he wasn't making as many tutorial videos as he used to. That sucked.

My eyes zoned in on a flashy white Jaguar parked up in the distance and a crowd of people surrounding it.

"I'll be back!" I told Mom as I darted off in the direction of the car.

"Come back, Simi!" she shouted, but I wasn't going to look back – I needed to see DJ Dan in the flesh. I could hear Mom's heels clicking faster as she tried to catch up with me until the sound suddenly stopped. I turned around and saw that she'd been approached by some paparazzi to pose with Dad. Mom was always more than happy to strike a pose for the cameras.

My heart was pumping with excitement as I glimpsed my idol. He was wearing a red baseball cap and a white tracksuit. Multiple gold chains and rings completed his rock star look. The crowd around him was swelling and people were jostling for a selfie or an autograph.

I hadn't been in the line for long when I felt Mom link arms with me. She dragged me off despite my best efforts to keep my feet firmly planted on the ground. I huffed as I reached the house.

Dad was getting a warm welcome, as usual. I found it weird. He was just Dad, but I could see how nervous people got when they met him. Some would just grin and stare at him, others would gush over his achievements, telling him they'd seen all his movies a million times over. Then there were those who'd grasp his hands in theirs and take ages to let go.

I spotted Producer Uncle over by a massive fountain in the hallway. That wasn't his real name, of course, but that's what I'd called him for as long as I could remember. He'd produced a few movies for Dad a couple of decades back and all had gone on to become big

successes. In fact, together they'd been known as the "hit factory." Mom often said that without Dad, Producer Uncle wouldn't be living in his mansion. I wondered whether that worked the other way around too. Would we be residents of the equally posh Jubilee Hills area without those mega movies he'd offered Dad?

Producer Uncle had pulled out all the stops for this gathering. No expense had been spared. The house had been decorated lavishly with balloons, flowers and twinkling fairy lights. Servers wearing neat black and white uniforms circled with fresh juices and canapes for the guests. The ladies – with their bright and blingy sarees – mingled with big, wide smiles and over-friendly expressions. The men relaxed on plush outdoor furniture by the swimming pool with ice-cold drinks.

Mom was now forcing me to do the rounds – a polite "Namaste" here, there and everywhere. "This is Simi," she began when introducing me to the adults who I had to adopt as my aunties and uncles – that's just how it was in India.

"Wow, she's grown so much!" said one lady who I swear I'd never seen before.

"She's at the Bollywood Academy, preparing for a career as an actress," Mom told another one of her acquaintances proudly.

"Actor, Mom, not actress," I corrected, but nobody took any notice.

"Ah, we hope she can fulfil all your ambitions," the lady replied. "Those not blessed with sons deserve to have the most successful daughters."

Ugh! I glared at the lady. How could attitudes like that still exist? I wasn't able to disrespect my elders by answering back but I bristled all the same.

As we continued doing the rounds, I thought how much I could do without all this. I wondered when I'd be able to slip back to the autograph line and what I'd ask DJ Dan to sign.

"Do you want to hang with us?"

I turned to see Producer Uncle's daughter, Bhavani, with her hair in a big bun, and wearing a lilac lehenga skirt, cute crop top and dupatta draped over it. Wow, I was totally underdressed.

"Yeah, sure," I replied, hoping she could introduce me to DJ Dan without me having to ask Dad to pull strings.

Bhavani was a couple of years older than me but I always felt like she was younger. Fashion sense aside, she was obsessed with toys and loved watching cartoons. As if to prove my point, she took me to a room in the house which was practically a toy shop. It was stacked with Lego kits, board games, a giant wooden dolls house and loads

 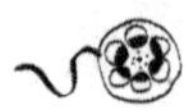

of kids going wild to see what they could find.

My eyes went straight to the piano.

"Can I try?" I asked.

She nodded before telling the younger children off for touching her collection of Barbie dolls. "Don't touch their hair," she said possessively. "The strands come loose."

The kids moved over to the dolls house while I made myself comfortable at the piano. I began playing a romantic song from a 1980s Bollywood movie. The original didn't feature the sounds of the piano but I'd created my own version of it at the age of seven. I'd improved it over the years and performed it multiple times during school assemblies for different age groups.

"Wow, this girl can play!"

I turned around sharply and my breath stopped at the sight of DJ Dan and a few of his friends standing in the doorway.

"That's Shyam's daughter," muttered one of the guys.

"*The* superstar Shyam?" DJ Dan asked.

His friend nodded.

DJ Dan's eyes lit up. "Oh wow, I'm your dad's biggest fan!" he gushed. "I grew up watching him. He's my idol!"

I didn't know what to make of that. How could DJ Dan – *my* idol – be telling me that my dad was *his* idol?

"Can you introduce me?" he asked.

Words weren't exactly tumbling out of my mouth and I was wondering whether this was the right moment to ask for his autograph but I didn't have a pen and didn't have anything to sign.

I nodded and stood up to lead the way. As we walked through the main hallway, I caught sight of Mom posing for more photos with a group of ladies who looked super rich with their sparkling jewelry and perfectly-manicured nails.

"There's Simi," Mom told them. I was determined not to stop or make eye contact.

"Oh wow, she has such big, black eyes – like an Indian goddess!" replied one of the older ladies with a silver-gray bun.

Mom threw her head back and laughed. "We have high hopes for Simi – in Bollywood not Tollywood."

I wished I could stop Mom from dissing the local film industry to the residents, even if Tollywood was smaller and less famous than Bollywood. And I wished they wouldn't talk about me as though I couldn't hear.

Mom wasn't quite as smiley when the same lady quipped: "Maybe you can manage her career, so you don't have to keep trying to get roles for yourself?"

Ouch.

I quickened my pace and found Dad sitting outside on the patio. He smiled when he saw me.

"Dad, this is DJ Dan," I said, relieved that I was now able to speak.

Dad stood up to shake his hand. "Hello, Dan. Is that your full name?"

"Danyal, sir," he replied. "Dan for short. I'm a huge fan. I've seen every single one of your movies. Over and over again."

Gosh, I would have thought Dan could have come up with something a little more original!

Dad nodded in acknowledgment. He was so casual about accepting praise. I guess he'd heard it so many times in his life, and he really didn't seem to get how much of a legend DJ Dan was.

As for me, it was sinking in how famous my father had been at his peak, which was a few years before I was born.

"Your daughter plays fine piano," Dan told Dad.

My stomach leaped with excitement. Most of the kids who'd been inside had followed us out, all Dan fans no doubt.

"Yes, Simi is an amazing pianist and a star cricket player," Dad chuckled. "But she'll be an even bigger movie star," he said proudly. "She's at the Bollywood

Academy – it's the best stage school out there."

Ugh, not Dad stealing Mom's line!

Dan raised his eyebrows as he looked at me. "Multi-talented I see."

"And," added Dad, "you'd better watch out as she's great at making music too. She has so many tunes on that thingy on her phone – what's it called?"

"It's just an app, Dad," I whispered, petrified that DJ Dan would want to hear one of my creations.

"Is that so?" asked Dan. "Maybe you want to show me? I'll play one. You have your cell?"

Gulp. I wasn't confident about playing anything but I didn't know how to get out of it. I pulled my phone from my pocket and opened the SoundCloud app.

"Choose a track and I'll hook you up to the speakers," he told me as my dad wandered off and left me to it.

"For real?" I asked.

"For real. Anything for Shyam's daughter," he laughed, showing off the metal grilles on his teeth.

I followed Dan to his podium and watched as he connected my phone to his speakers via Bluetooth. I pointed out my favorite song – the one Zeeshan always raved about. As the music began to blare from the humongous speakers, the ladies who'd been gathered inside started making their way out.

By now, it was totally dark. The water in the swimming pool had been completely still but was now rippling in the gentle evening breeze.

I saw Mom moving toward us, summoning me with her hand. She pointed to where Bhavani and the other girls had gathered. I shook my head and averted my gaze, focusing on DJ Dan who was really pumping up the volume now.

I pinched myself. Dan was playing one of my tunes and nodding his head along to the beat! My legs felt like Jell-O and I wondered if they'd give way from under me! Suddenly, DJ Dan was motioning me up into his booth. I didn't need to be asked twice. In fact, I was so eager to get there, I almost tripped on one of the steps leading up to it.

I was amazed at how DJ Dan had so quickly grabbed his audience's attention. Guests were edging forward, putting down their drinks and creating a dance floor of their own on the lawn in front of his booth. Older men were leaving their comfy wicker seats and pulling their wives onto the grass. Further back by the patio area, a group of teenagers had created a little boogie circle of their own. Some younger boys were crowding in front of the booth to dance – well, more like jump up and down. Adrenaline was surging through me – it was electrifying!

DJ Dan cranked up the sound. I watched his hands moving magically as he began mixing my track with a Bollywood golden oldie – how did he know that would work? Before I knew it, Dan was layering four tracks with so much ease and with the most mind-blowing results. His hands moved at lightning speed. There was no way I could layer like that but I was quite good at cross-fading – I'd learned the art of transitioning from one track to another from the YouTuber himself.

I glanced up and saw that Dad and Producer Uncle had moved closer and were clapping in rhythm. Govind, our cricket club manager, had also turned up and was chanting "Simi! Simi!" Mom looked less pleased but I didn't care. I'd deal with her later. The atmosphere in the yard was buzzing now, the party in full swing – thanks to my tune and DJ Dan!

When the song came to an end, I was sweating. DJ Dan put his thumbs up in appreciation, then grabbed his mic. "Wow, what a result! I don't usually let girls into my booth, but I made an exception for the daughter of the legendary Shyam Prasad!"

Uff.

I felt like the wind had been knocked out of me.

So that's all he had to say? Not that I'd composed an awesome tune but that I was my dad's daughter, and a

girl? What did my gender have to do with anything? His words felt like a punch in the stomach.

I had been well and truly cut down to size.

I looked up to see Mom indicating for me to get out of there. For the first time that evening, I was happy to do as she told me. I slipped out of the booth quickly and quietly.

Perhaps this wasn't the day I got DJ Dan's autograph after all.

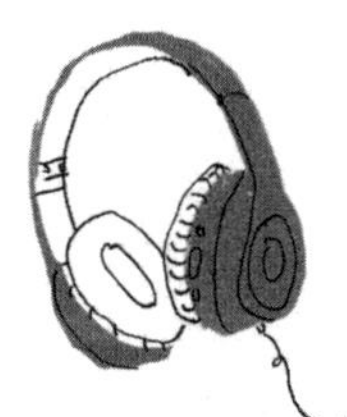

TAKE THREE

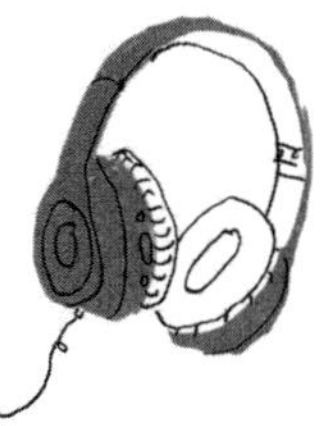

The last week of the summer break flew by and I was getting excited at the thought of seeing my school friends again. I'd pretty much managed to put DJ Dan's comments behind me, and when some of the kids at the party messaged me afterwards to say my tune was awesome, I was boosted.

At the start of the school year, Mom accompanied me for the 90-minute flight from Hyderabad to Mumbai. As we were about to exit Mumbai airport, she grabbed a copy of *Telugu Tinsel* magazine from the airport shop. Once aboard the ferry bound for Kohinoor Island, Mom eagerly flipped through the "Out and About" section, no doubt looking for images of herself.

"Oh, here's Mohan's birthday bash!" she enthused as she came across some pictures. Her eyes quickly scanned the page. She kept looking, then frowned a little. Mom lifted the magazine up close and then set it back down on her lap. She looked annoyed.

"What's up?" I asked. "There's Dad! Where are—?" Then it hit me. "Oh, they couldn't fit you in," I mumbled. "I guess the photo lens was only so wide."

"Why don't you just say it?" she snapped. "They cropped me out!"

I looked carefully at the selection of images again and Dad appeared in three photos, including one with DJ Dan. It was clear Mom hadn't made the final cut.

"It'll be nice to catch up with your old actor friends in Mumbai, won't it, Mom?" I said, trying to steer the conversation in a different direction.

"Old is the right word," she answered, before resting her head back and closing her eyes.

I went very quiet, not knowing what to do or say next. After a few moments, Mom opened her eyes and forced a small smile. "I hope you get the best opportunities, Simi. I miss you when you're at the Academy."

I reached out to hold her hand.

"You could just as easily have been training for a future in Telugu cinema and living at home," she added. "But we make these sacrifices for you because in India, nothing is bigger than Bollywood."

She kissed my forehead while I snuggled up against her arm, holding her tight for the final part of our journey.

*

TAKE THREE

Entering the famous wrought-iron gates of the Bollywood Academy, porters rushed out to grab my bags and load them onto a cart to take inside. It was a busy day for them – the parking lot was full and the reception area of the school looked like a hotel lobby with all the luggage lined up.

"Good afternoon, Mr. Pereira," said Mom, putting her hands together in a namaste gesture.

"Afternoon, Mrs. Prasad," replied the Vice Principal.

Mrs. Arora, the Principal, was talking to a small group of parents but she acknowledged Mom from a distance.

It always struck me how spotless and glistening the Academy was. I noticed new additions to the Smart Garden as we passed a window in one of the corridors, including trees with leaves that looked real and moved with the wind. I'd read in our Welcome Back newsletter that they were designed to maximize the sunlight they could capture to convert into energy for the Academy. That really *was* smart.

We quickly made our way to my dorm. I was eager to get settled in and catch up with my buddies. Joya and I would be staying in the same room as last year which was great as we had the most fantastic view across Kohinoor Island. We could see the Arabian Sea from one of the windows.

Joya and I got along really well even though we didn't have much in common. Her wall – covered with posters of all things Korean including K-pop and K-dramas – was in stark contrast to mine which featured sports personalities and rock stars.

"Now, you know what I'm going to say, don't you?" questioned Mom, settling my suitcase on top of my bed. She unzipped the case and began taking out some clothes.

"Leave it, Mom," I said. "You're tired. I can manage."

In truth, I was ready for her to leave so I wouldn't have to hear the "Focus on school and acting – not music and sports" lecture. And, of course, "Hang out with girls too, not always boys."

Mom checked her appearance in the long mirror on my wardrobe door, neatly applying some more powder and lipstick before we made our way back out to the driver.

"I'll be back in November for the midterm break, Mom," I said as she gave me a goodbye kiss. Her eyes began welling up, so she removed her gigantic sunglasses from her head and placed them over her face.

Joya appeared at the perfect moment, running out of her car to greet us. She looked so sweet in a flowy white skirt and white halterneck top. A high ponytail completed the look. "Don't worry, auntie," she said, noticing Mom's emotional state. "We were fine last year – we'll be fine this year too!"

Joya and I watched and waved from the steps of the reception area as her car rolled out of the famous gates.

"Freedom!" I screamed, hugging and high-fiving Joya. We giggled all the way back to our room, getting told off for running down the corridor by our dorm parent, Jannat. There was only one dorm parent on each floor but because she was at our end of the corridor, we often got the bulk of the reprimands.

Once inside our room, I hooked my phone up to my portable speaker to blast some tracks, and strummed my imaginary guitar.

"It's a bummer I couldn't bring my Yamaha keyboard to school," I said wistfully.

"Can you imagine the noise we'd make?" Joya commented. "Miss Jannat would be screaming all the time!"

We chuckled and Joya started humming away in the background. She had a beautiful voice and planned to become a Bollywood playback singer one day. Her parents were small-time singers in Calcutta who performed at local weddings and parties.

I often wondered why kids followed in the footsteps

of their parents. Ever since I could remember, I'd known that acting was my destiny. Was it because my biggest role models – my parents – were actors, or because they had subtly drummed it into me? Mom for sure nurtured a "Bollywood leading lady" ambition for me, maybe because she'd only ever had small, supporting roles.

"I can't wait to see the boys," I told Joya as we finished unpacking and headed down to eat. We looked around the dining hall.

"Boo!" came a voice from behind us.

I screamed in delight and wrapped Zeeshan in a hug. "Missed you, Zee!"

"Yeah, we can't hug like this on Zoom or Facetime, can we?" he replied before reaching out to embrace Joya.

Raktim waved at us as he walked in. He had a nice tan and somehow looked more grown-up than the last time I'd seen him. After another round of hugs, we went to the counter to grab some pizza and chips. We sat down to eat while watching the newbies – the Grade 6s – file in.

"Wow, they look so tiny!" I remarked. "Were we that small and innocent-looking last year?"

Zeeshan grabbed one of my pizza slices when I wasn't looking – something he did a lot – and I playfully punched him in the arm and promised to get him back.

"Guys, I have something to tell you!" I began when

we'd finished wolfing down our food. "I was waiting till I saw you in person..." I paused, maximizing the suspense. "Last week I met DJ Dan!"

"*What?!*"

"*No way!*"

I was bombarded with a chorus of exclamations.

My friends looked on in amazement as I filled them in on all the details.

"That's totally awesome!" said Zeeshan finally. "What was he like? Did you get a selfie? Did you get an autograph?" The questions came thick and fast.

"Well, Zee," I started, "after he shamed my gender in front of a couple hundred people, no, I didn't get an autograph or a selfie."

Zeeshan laughed. "I'm sure he meant no harm. You're lucky you got to go in his booth even though you *are* a girl."

"*What?!*" I exclaimed. "Why should being a girl bar me from his booth? What century are you guys living in? Why can't a girl make music?"

"Hey, come on! It's obvious I'm kidding," he shot back quickly, realizing I was offended.

And why wouldn't I be offended? Mom had already lectured me on the way home about dressing "like a boy" and doing "boy things," like hanging out with DJs.

Luckily, Dad had backed me up. "Be proud of her, Radhika. The universe has big plans for Simi," he'd said. "All those people who tell us we need a son – no, we don't. We're blessed to have a daughter who has all the qualities we desire in a boy *or* girl."

Aww.

We chatted for almost an hour before we were told by the dining hall staff to make our way back to our dorms. Enroute, we spotted a big crowd outside one of the classrooms.

"It's the Grade 8s," whispered Zeeshan. "That's Monica."

I gasped. She was taller than before, and she'd been pretty statuesque to start with! Monica was *the* star kid at our school. She'd even appeared in Bollywood Academy ads on TV over the summer.

"You're a star child like her," Zeeshan joked as we edged closer.

"No way, not even the same," I commented. "Tollywood ain't Bollywood and most people here haven't even heard of my dad." Zeeshan clearly loved winding me up, and it usually worked.

"What's this?" Raktim asked Monica as she handed him a leaflet.

"An opportunity you can't miss," she told him. "It's

your chance to perform live to millions around the world at the OBAs – the Official Bollywood Awards. I'm telling you, it's an incredible opportunity. It's being held at the Taj Mahal this year."

There were plenty of stage schools around the world but this was the only one that seemed to consistently and regularly give its students real-world opportunities. Monica and some other Grade 8s had starred in a massive hit called *Jigsaw* a few months earlier, as just one example. Passing students grabbed the flyers at breakneck speed. The excitement was real.

"Look – they want actors, singers, dancers, musicians," I said excitedly, looking up and down the list.

I decided to go for it. Mom would be over the moon to see me on stage at such a high-profile event.

I wanted to make her proud that I was following the path she had laid out for me.

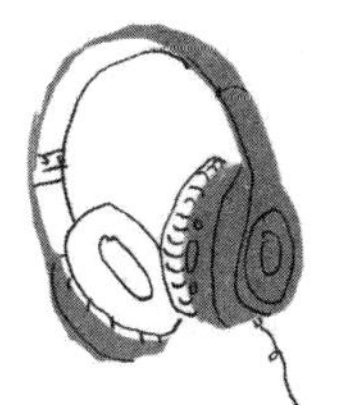

TAKE FOUR

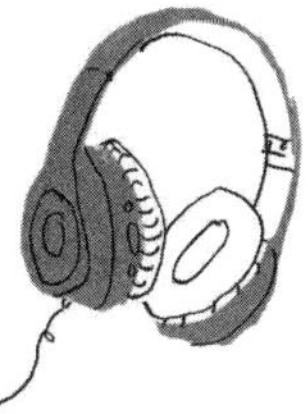

My feet were all tangled up. I was a terrible dancer.

"Simi!"

Uh oh, I thought to myself. Miss Patel, the dance teacher, who looked like she was 12-years-old herself with her tiny frame and baby face, was not impressed.

"Come on, you're not focusing." She called me up to the front to show everybody else how *not* to do it. "Simi is moving around on the balls of her feet. The foot needs to be flat." She banged her foot hard on the floor to demonstrate. Then the other one.

I knew that that was how it was done, I just could never remember. Mom had forced me to go to Bharatanatyam classes when I was younger but I kept making excuses like pretending I had stomachache, so she finally gave up.

I got it right eventually and I was relieved when Miss Patel let me re-join the others.

"I'll be glad to drop this subject," I told Joya after class as we headed off for a break.

"How can you drop dance?" she asked, grabbing cookies from her bag and passing one to me. "Dance is

essential for actors – especially in Bollywood."

"Is it?" I asked.

"Duh!" she replied, rolling her eyes. "Unless you want to work in Hollywood."

"I could use body doubles, couldn't I?" I joked. "Dad always uses stuntmen for his fight scenes."

Joya shook her head, laughing.

We went and sat on the grassy lawn beside the steps leading down from the Observatory – an awesome dome-shaped glass building with amazing views over Kohinoor Island. Joya pulled the OBAs leaflet out of her bag to scour the list. "What category are you entering, Sim?" she asked.

"The acting sketch," I told her. "Since that's what I plan to do in life, and what Mom would want, it makes sense. But I'm not that confident with it," I confessed. "Ever since I can remember, my parents have talked about my future acting career, but I'm beginning to wonder whether I'm a natural."

"You're only twelve! Don't be so hard on yourself," she replied, nudging me in the ribs.

"Yeah, you're right..." I thought of the Bollywood Academy logo: *We hone your talent so you can shine like a star*. "I guess there's still time. What are you entering?"

"Not sure," she said after a brief pause. Joya was busy

making a daisy chain, expertly cutting into the stems of the daisy with her fingernails and inserting the stalks into the holes. "I'd like to sing but I don't know if I want to perform on my own at such a big event."

I pondered for a moment and then caught sight of Zeeshan and Raktim further down the hill. They were playfighting. *I could teach them a few moves*, I thought to myself. I usually got the better of Dad when we wrestled.

"I know!" I said, sitting up. "How about you three enter as a band? For this one event, B-Tunes could be a trio. Here – look, it says 'Music Acts.'"

"Yes, yes, yes!" said Joya, grabbing the paper from me. "Genius idea, Sim!"

She bolted upright and rushed down to the boys to share the idea with them. They listened carefully, Raktim smiling throughout and Zeeshan nodding when she was done. I grabbed my bag and ran off to join them, conscious that it was almost time for our Hindi class.

"So what do you think?" I asked them.

"B-Tunes is gonna hit the big time!" beamed Zeeshan. "But what about you, Simi? We can't do it without you."

"Aww, that's sweet," I smiled. Zeeshan was the one who had asked me to join B-Tunes in the first semester of Grade 6. He had seen me play the piano in assembly and had found me during break to invite me. We hit it

off straight away. "I know Mom will want me to stick to acting for these big events," I explained. "Music is fine for fun, but it's not a career for me."

"Well, yeah, that's always been clear," said Zeeshan. "As long as you promise to rehearse with us and help us out. You know we get stuck without you."

"Deal," I said, shaking Zeeshan's hand.

"Practice after school?" asked Raktim.

"Try to stop me!" I laughed before promising to meet them later.

We dashed back inside for our next class. Because we had new schedules and different classrooms in Grade 7, I found it a bit stressful getting to the right place at the right time. The day just seemed that much busier and before I knew it, it was over.

"Phew!" I slumped down in the plush velvet armchair in the lounge of the Noise Zone – Bollywood Academy's music studio – while Zeeshan signed in on the digital monitor at the entrance. This was a space that was available to all students but we had to book sessions on the Academy app.

Like everything else in this school, the Noise Zone was top-of-the-line. It had every piece of technology you could ever need to record whatever type of music you wanted to.

On one side was the producer's booth with a massive mixing console. There were plenty of computers too with an assortment of headphones. On the other side were smaller isolation booths designed for different musical instruments. A glass wall at the end of the room led to the main studio – a massive space with a multitude of instruments including a piano, violins, drums, electronic keyboards, guitars, sitars and tabla. There was a row of fixed seating for small audiences at one end. To me, it was the best place in the whole of the Academy.

"We don't have much time, guys. Joya, go into the vocal booth, please," I instructed. She headed off while Zeeshan strummed his guitar and Raktim took control of the drums.

The boys weren't playing in time so I stood up to intervene.

"Zeeshan and Rakhtim, you're starting off at different tempos... You need to really listen to each other to stay in sync."

They nodded and, thankfully, got into the zone. Just a few simple tweaks made all the difference. Joya raised the energy in her vocals. Zeeshan moved his head rhythmically and struck the chords in perfect tune.

"Yeah! Much better!" said Zeeshan as our jamming session ended. "Thanks, Simi," he added.

We fist-bumped.

"When are the actual auditions for the OBAs?" I asked.

"Mid-September, dost," replied Raktim. I always smiled when he called me "friend" in Hindi.

While Joya, Zeeshan and I knew what we wanted to do in the industry, Raktim was undecided. He said he could just as easily opt to be a cinematographer as he could a dialogue writer or film director. His dad was extremely wealthy with a thriving food export company. Raktim could even join the family business.

"What about your audition, Sim?" asked Zeeshan. "You'd better make time for that too."

I nodded. I loved being with B-Tunes but I was all too aware that I was at the Academy to train to be an actor. Maybe if I prioritized acting, it would come more naturally to me. Perhaps I would like it more and feel more comfortable.

Making music a secondary thing in my life wasn't going to be easy, I discovered. I was usually so excited about music class with our teacher Mr. Joshi but the following day, I felt a tinge of sadness as I decided to take a back seat.

"Staccato is when each note is detached from the next. Think sharp, quick motions," said Mr. Joshi, striking the keys of the piano without letting the sound vibrate longer than the time it took him to touch the keys.

"Who would like to demonstrate?" he asked, peering over the top of his black, thick-rimmed glasses. Mr. Joshi had a small bald patch which shone when he got too warm. Seeing him wipe his head with a handkerchief was a common sight.

I saw him looking at me but my hand didn't go up. I lowered my head.

A girl named Naila was called up to the front to play. She tried hard, but she held the notes too long. A simple error but a crucial one.

Mr. Joshi sighed. "Practice makes perfect, Naila," he said.

Naila nodded and duly took her seat. Nobody else raised their hand, probably worried that they'd also get it wrong. I told myself I wouldn't do this, but I slowly put my hand up. Mr. Joshi smiled. I walked to the front of the music room where the majestic Steinway & Sons black piano sat. My heart raced as I approached it.

I sat down and caressed the keys of the piano, choosing to play a spikey tune full of quick detached notes to demonstrate the staccato. I started slowly and then built speed and pace until I hit a crescendo. This was so easy for me. And so enjoyable.

"Well done, Simi!" Mr. Joshi clapped when I had finished. He looked elated, like a proud parent. I was happy that he was pleased but I made sure I didn't look at Naila as I didn't want her to feel bad.

"That's everyone's homework for the week," Mr. Joshi said, looking at the clock. "Pick a melody – your own or someone else's – and practice staccato. I'll be listening to all of you next week and then we move to legato!"

As soon as the bell went, the silence was broken by the sounds of students gathering their belongings and chattering with friends as they filed out of the door.

"Simi," Mr. Joshi called as I was heading out. "Can I have a word?"

I walked over to him.

"Is everything alright?" he asked, dabbing his head with his handkerchief. "You barely glanced up the whole class and, until the very end, you didn't raise your hand for a single question."

"Sorry, sir," I said. "I'm just trying to focus on the things I'm here to study – like drama and all the academic subjects like math and science. I think music is distracting me a little."

Mr. Joshi looked puzzled. "Why would you not put effort into a subject when you enjoy it and have natural talent?" he asked.

I shrugged my shoulders.

"Not trying in one subject won't make you better at another one," he chuckled. "In fact, excel at music and you'll gain confidence to excel in other subjects too. Winning is addictive. Once you start, you won't want to stop."

He had a point. "Yes, sir, I understand."

"Plus music is a subject that can give you a certification. Don't think it's meaningless. Any time you want to practice the piano, use the one in the Performance Hall if it's available."

I thanked Mr. Joshi again – that was a real privilege. I promised him I'd be more engaged next time.

As I was leaving, he said: "I'm glad, Simi. I would hate to lose my best student."

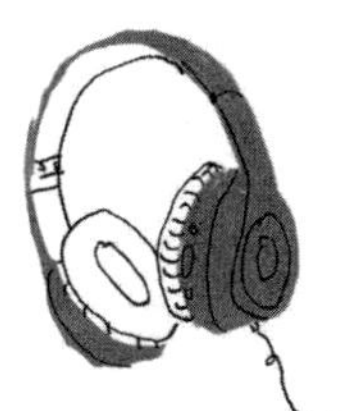

TAKE FIVE

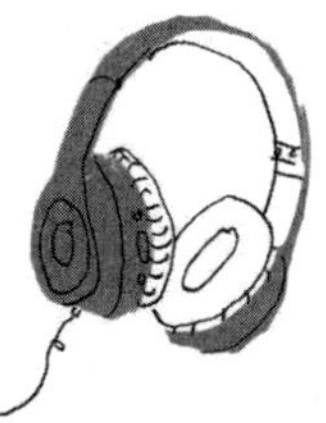

"No! I didn't steal the money!" I shouted.

It was the day of the OBA drama auditions and I was really going for it.

"You're always accusing me of things," I yelled. "First, you said I lied. Then, you told me I tricked you. And now, you're calling me a thief!" I put my head in my hands and sobbed dramatically.

"Hmm," said Miss Takkar, Head of Drama. She didn't look pleased. She glanced over at her assistant judges, made up of two teachers and two Grade 8 students who were avoiding making eye contact with me.

Marc Fernandez and Bela Khanna were mini celebs at the Academy since the runaway success of their movie *Jigsaw*. Bela had followed it up with a massive role in a movie directed by Om Shankara, one of India's star directors.

I could guess what they were thinking. When I was reading out that dialogue from the sheet Miss Takkar had given me, I was stumbling over words and shouting rather than really feeling the part. Maybe I was too self-conscious? I'd spent most of Grade 6 avoiding auditions

and here I was now, doing badly at one in front of the coolest kids in school.

“The emotions have to come from within,” said Miss Takkar, extending her hands for emphasis. “You must get inside your character’s head, put yourself in their shoes. Imagine what they are going through – feel their pain, share in their joy, express it freely, without limitations or embarrassment.”

Hmm. Maybe that was my issue with drama. I found it hard to act without feeling a little silly.

“Okay then, let’s try some comedy,” offered Miss T in an encouraging tone. “The organizers of the OBAs want to add humor to one of the sketches by getting some students to do physical stunts while wearing comic expressions.”

She straightened up in her chair. I noticed that Miss Takkar was somehow looking younger than she used to. There were golden highlights in her hair.

“Run over to the stage behind you, pretend to slip on a banana skin and rub your back as though you’ve hurt yourself. Then cry in a humorous fashion.”

Bela laughed. “Aha, like our catwalk show at the *Jigsaw* premier,” she said to Marc.

I didn’t know what she was talking about, but this comic thing sounded far easier than serious acting. I sprinted to the stage, pushed one leg out, waved my arms around and fell. I put on an over-the-top slapstick expression, made fists with my hands, rubbed my eyes, and opened my mouth wide to simulate crying.

Somehow, it made Miss Takkar smile. "Yes, much better, Simi. Comedy may be your forte."

Bela clapped and smiled sweetly at me. Marc gave me the thumbs-up. I blushed.

I politely thanked the panel, then walked back out, feeling no other emotion than relief that it was over.

I was super hungry but my watch was telling me that there was still time to catch B-Tunes rehearsing. I darted down to the Noise Zone and gently tapped on the door. A staff member let me in. Inside, Raktim was struggling with the sound.

"What's up?" I asked.

He smiled when he saw me, but I knew he was stressed from the way he was repeatedly tapping his foot on the floor. "I can't seem to get it right," he said. "It's more like noise than music."

"Here, let me have a go."

I fiddled with the bass and treble knobs. Suddenly, the music wasn't drowning out Joya's sweet vocals anymore.

"Go again, Joya," I said.

She closed her eyes and sang from the top.

"It's much better but something still isn't right," said Zeeshan, airing his frustration. He picked up his guitar and began plucking again.

"He's right. It's not working," agreed Raktim.

Zeeshan put the guitar down angrily. "I can't get the melody right."

Joya and Raktim looked worried. Zeeshan started clicking his fingers and then tapping his feet. He began singing to the beat, trying to work up a rhythm, but it just wasn't happening.

"Let's call it a day," suggested Raktim, moving off toward the sofa. "Sometimes it's best to sleep on it. We can start afresh tomorrow."

"How can we do it tomorrow, Mr. Positivity?" Zeeshan snapped. "Tomorrow is the audition! What if we can't get it right tomorrow? The chance will be gone!"

Joya sat quietly on the sofa, playing with her hair. She looked tense. "I don't think it's that bad."

"Of course it's bad!" countered Zeeshan. "It's too repetitive. The ending doesn't work!"

"How about if we don't try to compose an original tune. We could be a tribute band?"

Zeeshan looked at Joya in disbelief. "*You* can be a tribute band – no way *I'm* going to do that if I want to be a film composer in future. This is my chance to shine!"

There was a lot of tension in the air. I walked over to the vending machine and used my fingerprint to buy myself a can of orange soda. I took a few cooling gulps.

"Okay, I think I have it," I announced, wiping my mouth.

They all looked at me, hopefully.

"Maybe I can see it because I'm a bit more removed from it."

"See what?" asked Zeeshan.

"It's not working because there's no bridge. And I think a key change would really help. Remember what Mr. Joshi told us: 'Leave a surprising or interesting moment for the listener.' It sounds a bit flat because there's no climax."

They all looked at me, as if waiting for more.

"Here, like this." I sang the chorus and then improvised a few lines of melody to transition the song toward a key change, building up to the final chorus.

There was no reaction.

"It needs a bit of work, of course," I said modestly, before singing the bridge again, adapting it a bit as I did until I was more comfortable with it.

This time, Joya started humming along so I repeated it a little louder. The time after that, she began singing. A smile spread across her face. I could also see the

expression on Zeeshan's face changing. He picked up his guitar and began strumming while I clapped along. Joya carried on singing. Raktim gently banged on the table to create a drum beat.

We did it a few more times before Raktim changed the order of a few words and went over to the drums, hammering out the new section. We had another go and it finally clicked into place.

"We're singing from our heart, *dil se*, *dil se*," sang Joya. "This song is just for you-uu, *dil se*, *dil se*."

Zeeshan played loudly and joyously. Raktim looked pleased at his clever combination of English and Hindi words in the chorus.

I smiled as I watched them rehearse. I was so proud of my bandmates. I was also proud of myself, for being able to help them in their time of need. We were a true team.

When they told me the following day that their audition had gone well, I gave them big, tight hugs and secretly claimed some of the credit for it.

Now, we just needed to find out whether we would make it through to perform at the live event at the Taj Mahal.

*

TAKE FIVE

Raktim, Joya and Zeeshan were already there when I burst into the Games Room the following evening after the final bell.

"You're late!" Joya told me.

"Sorry, guys," I said, taking off my hoodie. I was sweating from running so fast from the other side of the school. "Mr. Khan asked me to try out for the soccer team."

"Wow, check you!" smiled Zeeshan, pleased but obviously taken aback. It wasn't just a team for girls – I was trying out for the boys' soccer team.

"And we have news too," he announced.

"News?" I asked. "We? Who is 'we'?"

"We – as in B-Tunes," explained Joya.

"And the news is – we're in!" yelled Raktim.

"You got chosen? For the OBAs?"

"Yes we did – and you helped us, Sim!" said Zeeshan. "Your new ending helped a lot. I could see the judges nodding along when we got to the key change."

I went over to hugratulate them one by one, struggling to put on a genuine smile. I was delighted, of course, but hurt that they hadn't waited for me before they checked the email.

"Your turn now, dost," Raktim said, turning his laptop toward me. "Log in and check."

Joya crossed her fingers for me and I quickly entered my username and password. I felt a little pressure, simply because they were all staring at the screen. I desperately hoped I wouldn't be the one who got rejected.

I clicked on the email titled "Official Bollywood Awards: Audition Result."

"Yes!" Zeeshan was quicker off the mark than I was. "Hugratulations, Simi!" he shouted.

I laughed. I was so relieved.

"Yay! We're all going to Agra!" whooped Joya, giving me a kiss on the cheek.

Raktim and I did our special high-low, side-to-side fist bump.

We were attracting quite a lot of attention but we didn't care. I was over the moon at the thought of being on stage with actual Bollywood stars and getting to be seen on TV in thousands of homes across India and around the world!

The first person who came to mind was Mom. I couldn't wait any longer. I left B-Tunes in the Games Room and ran outside to Facetime my parents.

"I told you! The universe has big plans for you!" Dad said.

"Well done, Simi. *Mmmmwaaah!*" Mom gushed, before reeling off tips on how I should and shouldn't behave on and off stage. "Be confident and smile even though you may feel nervous. Practice your part beforehand and always face and look into the cameras if they're pointing at you."

"Don't worry, Mom, we'll get plenty of instructions from the school," I told her. "We start rehearsing tomorrow."

I didn't know what to expect from rehearsals but it was good to hear from our choreographer, Dilip, the next day that it wasn't going to be all work and no play.

"It's a fun segment. You'll be put into pairs for your routines," Dilip told us. He was quite young – mid-twenties was my guess. His tight black training tights and fitted T-shirt highlighted how athletic he was.

"There's ten of you in my group so please line up here, two by two," he added, pointing to the side of the Dance Hall that had mirrors along the wall. "Boys with boys and girls with girls."

There's a surprise, I thought to myself. But my quick math told me that Dilip's scheme was going to come undone with five girls and five boys.

"Sir," said a girl named Narinder, raising her hand. "Can Nuzhat and I please be paired together at the front? We want to go on first."

"I don't see why not," said Dilip.

Narinder and Nuzhat couldn't have smiled bigger smiles if they'd tried. The girls probably weren't related, but they looked very similar with a medium-brown skin tone and long dark hair, trimmed to the waist. They also wore similar clothes when not in uniform: skinny blue jeans, white sneakers, and crop tops just about long enough not to violate the rules of the Academy.

"This is not an 'acting sketch' per se," Dilip explained. "On the day, two actors who are making their movie debut this year will be singing and dancing together. Then, you guys will come onto the stage, in twos, and distract them with your own unique skills."

"We're gymnasts, sir!" boasted Narinder.

"Excellent!" Dilip was delighted. "So you could go on stage and synchronize cartwheels, backflips or similar."

The girls whispered something to each other and then took a few minutes to stretch and warm up before taking to the floor to demonstrate some of their talents. Impressive, I admitted to myself. Pointy toes, good core strength, and very well coordinated.

Dilip then did the same thing with the next three pairs – one more set of girls and two of boys – until only two of us were left: me and a Grade 8 student called Ajay Banerjee. I remembered his face from the movie *Jigsaw* although he'd had an itsy-bitsy role. Ajay was one of the few boys at school with a buzz cut.

"I think you and Ajay will fit together nicely," Dilip said to me.

A girl behind me laughed. "That's right – Simi's one of the boys."

I blushed but didn't turn around. I hoped nobody else had heard her.

As Ajay and I moved to one side to form our pair, I wondered why Dilip thought I would "fit together nicely" with Ajay. Did he think I acted like a boy? Worse still, *look* like one? He didn't know I played sports, after all.

Ajay smiled at me. I returned the gesture. "I've seen you doing kickups on the soccer field," he said. "You're good at soccer tricks."

"Thanks," I replied. I was surprised and flattered that he recognized me.

"I asked Mr. Khan to invite you for a tryout."

"Oh!" I exclaimed. "That was you?"

"Yep," he confessed. "How about we do an act with soccer tricks?"

I paused, then nodded. I'd love it, but Mom would hit the roof!

"What an original idea!" exclaimed Dilip when we told him. "That would be really entertaining. I've never seen that at a movie awards show before either. Please,

go ahead." Dilip wasn't actually doing very much choreographing, I realized. He was literally making us do stuff we were already good at. Hmm, *smart*.

Ajay and I walked to the storage area in the sports hall to pick up a couple of soccer balls. As we made our way back, I heard some familiar voices. Up ahead, Zeeshan, Raktim and Joya were rushing off in the direction of the Noise Zone.

"That's my band!" I told Ajay proudly. "B-Tunes – short for Bollywood Tunes. They're performing together at the OBAs."

"Oh, you're in a band?" he asked. "That's cool. Do you play instruments?"

I nodded. "Piano and keyboard mainly. I can play the guitar too but not as well as Zeeshan. And a little bit of violin. I really love violins but I've never had any tutoring. I make lots of music using apps like SoundCloud."

"Why didn't you enter with your band then?" Ajay asked.

"Haha, good question!" I laughed. "Music is just a hobby. I'm here to become an actor, so I had to go for the acting audition." I paused. "There isn't much acting involved though, is there?"

"Tell me about it!" Ajay agreed. "Oh well. We'll be

seen by millions of people. And we can have fun playing soccer, right?"

I liked this guy. For some reason, I always ended up making friends with boys, much to my mom's annoyance.

I was looking forward to four weeks of rehearsals with Ajay before the event in mid-October. But I also felt sad that I wouldn't be spending so much time with B-Tunes. Was this the moment we came to a fork in the road? I wasn't sure I was ready for it.

When the weekend came around, I was glad. A get-together with B-Tunes was just what I needed.

"This Bollywood awards show is giving me mixed emotions," I told Joya as I brushed my teeth on Saturday morning.

"Why?" she asked from the bedroom. I poked my head around the bathroom door. She was wearing one of her loom band ankle bracelets and was painting her toenails in rainbow colors to match.

"'Cause even though I enjoy rehearsals with Ajay, I also want to be with you guys. It's weird."

"Oh!" exclaimed Joya, blowing at her feet to make the varnish dry quicker. "We're not doing anything different," she added, before breaking off to hum a tune. "It's the same song."

"Zeeshan suggested I livestream your rehearsal while I'm in my rehearsal," I told Joya. "So I could be at both."

Joya stopped what she was doing and stood up straight. "Are you serious?"

I grinned mischievously.

"That is ridiculous! You know you could lose your space at the event if they find out? You're not even supposed to have your phone in rehearsals. BA rules still apply, you know."

She had a point. What was I thinking?

Joya took a seat at her desk to paint her fingernails the same colors. "You and Zee are joined at the hip – we all know that, Simi. But don't agree to all of his crazy schemes."

I felt a little small. A little stupid. She was right of course, but I would have liked her to say something like: "Yeah, Simi, we miss you too. Come and rehearse with us. Perform with us."

But why would she say that? I was the one who had decided to pursue acting.

I had to take consolation from the fact that there were only three weeks left before the show, and after that, there would be nothing to stop B-Tunes being a quartet once more.

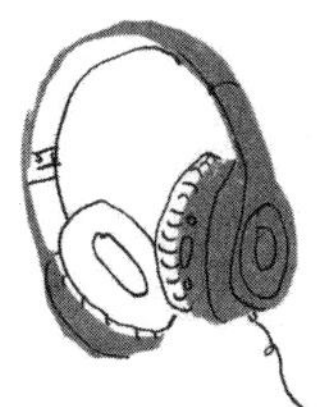

TAKE SIX

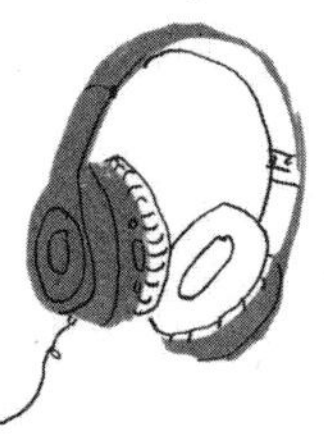

This was it.

About 2 board the plane! I texted our family WhatsApp group.

Take care, Simi. I'll be looking for you on stage! replied Mom.

Go kill it! said Dad. *Show the Northerners what a South Indian girl can do!*

That made me laugh.

I'd given all my documents to Dilip who was in charge of our group of ten. There were forty BA kids traveling, including my B-Tunes buddies who were taking the flight after me, to my mild annoyance. But I'd just spotted Ajay in the line so I went and stood next to him.

"Hey, Simi," he smiled. "Excited?"

I nodded. "Yeah – and scared that I'll mess up the act. My timing for the knee catches was off this morning but I think I was rushing it."

"Don't worry, Simi! After all, you're only performing live on stage in front of *millions of people...*"

My stomach did a kickup of its own.

"Just kidding!" he grinned. "I've seen you control a

ball. You'll be great."

"Well, I hope so," I replied.

I caught sight of Narinder and Nuzhat ahead of us. Both were wearing pink velour sweatsuits with some blingy writing up the left leg of the pants. Despite seeing each other weekly during rehearsals, they still hadn't acknowledged me and I hadn't spoken to them either. It was like we were invisible to one another.

My main motivation for this event, after seeing the Taj Mahal, was to make Mom happy. I felt like I'd disappointed her on so many occasions with my unconventional choices and hobbies. This was my chance to make her see I was on the path to Bollywood success at last!

The only problem now was that I hadn't told her I'd be playing soccer on stage. I mean, how did it even come to this? I was happy about it, but I could also imagine what Mom would say to me after the show. I felt nervous just thinking about it.

Having Ajay sit next to me on the plane was a nice distraction.

"What do your parents do?" I asked him.

"My mom passed away," he revealed candidly.

"Oh," was all I could think to say. I didn't expect that at all and felt sad to hear it. "Sorry."

"Thanks. It was when I was young. It's just me, my brother and Dad who works in banking. Pretty boring really."

It might be boring but it told me that Ajay's dad must be pretty wealthy. Most of the people at the Academy were, I guess. You had to be, to afford the tuition.

"Do you miss your mom?" I asked as we shifted a few steps toward the check-in desk.

"Yeah, of course," he replied. "I was just seven."

"I always listen to music when I want to stop thinking about sad things or when I want to change my mood," I informed him. "If you're feeling a bit down, you can change how you feel with happy music."

"That makes sense," he said noncommittally.

"Try it. Next time you're low, listen to music. Like *really* listen to it. Listen to all the different melodies, instruments and vocals. It can completely change your mood, maybe in the same way that exercise can."

"Hmm, I'll try it," he said politely. Maybe he thought I was crazy, I wasn't sure. I wanted to prove it to him. When we were on the plane, I took out my phone, clicked on Spotify and chose an uplifting song. I passed it to him with my AirPods.

"Listen, like I told you to."

Ajay listened for a few moments. I could tell he was

focusing hard, and after a while it seemed as if he had gotten lost in the song – he had closed his eyes and looked completely relaxed. I jolted him when I thought he was falling asleep.

He passed the AirPods back to me and smiled. "I get what you mean. I do listen to music but, yeah, maybe that's the first time I've truly heard it. Thanks."

"Oh, no need to thank me," I replied. "We can get so much more out of music if we just concentrate a bit more."

We spent the two hours on board discussing our favorite tunes and other hobbies. He also told me about his experience on film sets. The time flew by and before I knew it, we'd touched down.

A team of well-dressed people were waiting for us at Agra airport as we walked from the baggage reclaim area to the Arrivals Lounge. We headed for the person with a sign saying "BA: Dilip's Team."

Dilip, sporting a royal blue sweatsuit, took attendance and did a headcount. Before too long, we were on our way to our accommodation – a boutique hotel called the Agra Villas Resort. It wasn't very big but it was hands down the prettiest place I had ever stayed in. In the center of the small complex was an in-ground swimming pool. And in the center of that stood a tree decorated with pretty lights. Beautiful one-story cottages surrounded the pool.

Narinder and Nuzhat had already snapped ten selfies before we'd even checked in. If Joya had been with me, we would probably have done the same.

"Haha, that's girls for you," laughed Ajay as he watched them. I gave him one of my serious looks. "Just kidding," he smiled. "As a sporty girl, you can be considered one of the boys."

"Liking sports doesn't make me a boy!" I told him. "I'm just a girl who happens to like sports."

"And that's one of the best things about you," he said.

I felt a warm glow overtake my irritation. I was secretly pleased that such a popular Grade 8 boy was praising me.

We walked around a little, taking in all the detail. I loved the patterned driveway created from colorful marble tiles, lined with trees and a peacock fountain. I spotted a luxury wooden swing with a ruby red silk cushion that was big enough for two people to lie on.

"Wow!" shouted one of the boys in our group. "Can't wait to chill there."

"We're only here for two days so there will be no time for chilling," said Dilip, urging us to move toward the reception desk. As expected, loud groans echoed

around the courtyard. He looked at a sheet of paper the receptionist handed him.

"You and Ajay will have single rooms," Dilip said, pointing at me. "Everyone else gets a double room with their stage partner."

I didn't mind. In fact, it was cool to have my own space. I Facetimed Mom and Dad as soon as I got in.

"Don't hold back and don't overact," Mom instructed. "This is a big deal. You don't want things to go wrong in a live performance. That could stick for life," she said.

"Like a missed penalty in a soccer game," Dad chuckled.

I giggled.

"And make sure you put the right amount of emotion into...errr...it," Mom continued. "Actually, you haven't told us what you'll be doing on stage! A song and dance performance or a sketch? I've done both—"

"Oh, they're calling us now for dinner," I cut in. "Gotta go, bye!"

Phew, I thought. I really didn't want to have that conversation with Mom right now.

I walked over to the window to close the curtains and my jaw almost hit the floor when I saw the tip of the Taj Mahal! I eagerly snapped photos of it and sent it to my friends and family – including B-Tunes who told me they were on their way from the airport.

I'd seen photos of this super famous landmark in my history class and in the media for as long as I could remember. We even had a miniature sculpture of it in our back yard by the fountain. I couldn't believe I was so close to the real thing. I was determined to make the most of this experience even if it was going to be a whirlwind tour.

*

The next morning, bright and early, we were rushed through breakfast and into the minibus to be transported to a dress rehearsal on the specially erected stage outside the Taj.

"Simi," said Dilip, jolting me out of my thoughts as I stood staring at the magnificent 17th century building that stood tall, proud and immaculate in front of me. With its perfectly symmetrical white marble design, inlayed with precious stones, I could see why it was one of the Seven Wonders of the World.

The lighting technicians were shining laser beams up onto the stage which were in turn creating a spectacular light show on the Taj Mahal. Even in the bright light of day, the whole setup was dazzling.

"Here's your costume," said Dilip, handing me a folded-up package. He pointed to the area that was labeled "Dressing Rooms." I wasn't quite sure what I would be wearing but I could tell it was fully sequined and sparkling.

I noticed all the "Sponsored by Bollywood Academy" billboards being put up.

"Are we sponsoring this event?" I asked him. He nodded, looking around at the teams of people rushing around putting up the ads.

"Oh, now it makes sense."

"What does?" questioned Ajay, joining us.

"I was just wondering why such a national awards ceremony would want to use kids to do these little acts... plus all the way from Mumbai. Like there are no kids near Agra?"

Ajay laughed, his eyes doing that cute thing of almost disappearing into his face as he did so.

"Sponsored by us, so featuring us," he commented. "But don't forget, we have some stars at our school too."

He pointed.

On stage, obviously ready for their dress rehearsal, were the child stars of *Jigsaw* – surprise hit of the year. Monica, Bela, Marc, Shamim and Deepa were discussing something with the camera crew.

Shamim beckoned to Ajay.

"Gotta go. I'm needed over there too!" Ajay told me. "I'll be back for our routine."

Dilip gave Ajay permission to go and I went off to get changed. When I emerged again – wearing my sequined soccer uniform complete with jazzy matching socks – he told me to practice on one side of the stage until Ajay was ready to join me.

My outfit had my name and the number 7 – to show my school grade I guess – emblazoned on the back, and the words Bollywood Academy on the front under a round BA logo. I didn't usually wear such flashy stuff but I kind of liked it. Dilip gave me a soccer ball and handed out all the relevant props to the other kids.

I don't think I sat down again after that moment. We were literally made to rehearse over and over again for the rest of the day.

"We keep repeating the same stuff but we haven't had a chance to rehearse with the actual Bollywood stars!" moaned Narinder.

"You don't need to," said Dilip. "It's all going to work perfectly because they just happen to be on the stage when you perform. None of you are actually performing with them. Think of it as performing *for* them."

They both looked thoroughly fed up. Nuzhat crossed

her arms angrily.

"My feet hurt!" I complained to Ajay. He was wearing a similar outfit to mine but had a number 8 on the back of his shirt. "Especially my toes, from all the kickups over the past month."

"Mine too, but it's just for today," he reminded me. "A few more hours."

"Once the adrenaline kicks in, you'll be fine, Simi," Dilip added.

I hoped he was right. I was hobbling by the time rehearsals were over and we were told to line up by the stage ready for the show to begin.

"I can't believe how quickly they put together this whole stage and setting," Miss Takkar said to Dilip as we waited behind the black curtain.

Although my feet were sore, I wasn't nervous. I was excited at the chance of being on stage and eager to show off my skills.

Still, we couldn't avoid a little hitch. Nuzhat, who had been full of confidence ever since I'd set eyes on her, suddenly had an attack of nerves. She was sitting on the bottom step that led to the stage, shaking.

"Just breathe," Miss Takkar told her, holding her hands. "Maybe we should get a doctor," she whispered to Dilip with a worried look.

One of the medics rushed across to check her over. "It's a panic attack," he told Miss Takkar.

I had an idea.

I ran over to my backpack and grabbed my phone and AirPods. "Here, Nuzhat," I whispered, "listen to some music. It will take your mind off things."

She looked up at me, her face white with fear.

"Good idea," agreed Miss Takkar, snatching them off me. "Close your eyes and put these in."

We chose a soothing melody, hoping it would help her block out all the sounds and activity. There was a lot going on. People were dashing about, large cameras were getting ready for action and from the side of the curtain, I could see the audience filing in. It was a little overwhelming.

Miss Takkar smiled at me as she saw Nuzhat regaining color in her cheeks. She seemed to be breathing more calmly now too.

"Look – it's SriLata!" someone screamed. I turned around. Bollywood's Number 1 female actor had been called on stage to open the show.

"Almost time!" whispered Miss Takkar, careful that she didn't create more panic in Nuzhat who still had her eyes closed.

Watching the servers carrying platters of starters to

serve to guests seated at the round tables was making my mouth water. Pani puri, dahi vada and kachori were traditional Indian street foods but served up on big fancy plates like that with a sprig of mint on the side, they looked fit for a maharajah! Still, I'd have to wait.

Laser lights were now being beamed into the sky, casting rainbow colors over the Taj Mahal which stood out majestically against the night sky. What an awesome sight!

SriLata, wearing a heavily patterned saree, entered the stage to rapturous applause and began thanking everyone for coming.

I could see Zeeshan, Raktim and Joya standing on the other side of the backstage area. I waved. Joya didn't see me but the boys raised their arms and dabbed at me so I dabbed back, trying to stifle a giggle. I started doing a robot dance to make them laugh but realized they'd already turned their attention away from me. I frowned. It was hard not to feel a little lonely, a bit left out. I wished we could have been in this together.

I was shaken out of these thoughts when I heard the words "Bollywood Academy." SriLata must have finished her speech because she had been replaced on stage by a male host I didn't recognize.

"Thank you to our sponsor – the biggest and best

stage school in the east!" he boomed, before calling upcoming actors Sahil and Aarushi onto the stage.

"Okay, it's showtime," a friendly young lady told us. Dilip came and checked we were all in position and once the music started, Nuzhat – who was now a lot calmer – took to the stage with Narinder.

The Bollywood Academy logo flashed up on the giant screen as the girls stormed the stage to show off their gymnastics skills. Sahil and Aarushi watched with mock open mouths as they flawlessly carried out their routine – a few twirls and cartwheels, followed by a series of acrobatic dance moves. The act was being received really well, judging by the audience response.

I took a deep breath and squeezed Ajay's arm as we stood in line to follow on, soccer balls in our hands. My stomach was fluttering again, though more with excitement than nerves.

We walked onto the stage with full swagger. Sahil and Aarushi looked straight at us. Sahil grabbed a mic and shouted: "Show us what you've got!"

Ajay and I gave each other the signal we'd practiced and started performing our synchronized soccer kickups followed by a trick known as "around the world" where we kicked the ball up and circled around it with our foot while it was still in the air. Our final act, and my favorite

part, was the "rainbow flick" where we maneuvered the ball behind our backs and over our heads to the sides of the stage. The crowd was going wild for us and I was loving it! More than anything, I was relieved that neither of us had dropped the ball as we sauntered off stage and the next pair raced on.

It wasn't until I made my way into the wings that I started brooding over what Mom must be thinking right now. Of all the things she wouldn't have wanted me to do – kick a soccer ball around on stage would be the top one!

"Well done!" said Dilip enthusiastically. He gave me a fatherly pat on the head and fist-bumped Ajay.

We brushed past Bela, Monica and co. who were ready to go on stage to be interviewed by the host. "You were amazing," Monica whispered to me. "I'm telling you, girl, you have some skills!" I smiled back at her, feeling proud.

"You can watch the rest of the show with the other guests now," Dilip told us. He led us to our reserved seating a couple of rows from the front, with a great view of the stage and the Taj. Ajay stayed back to join the Grade 8s for the on-stage interview about *Jigsaw*.

"Woohoo! Go Ajay!" I yelled from my seat as the cast and crew of *Jigsaw* walked on. Nuzhat and Narinder turned to look at me and giggled but I wasn't bothered. It made me feel so proud to see my friend up there.

The host – who I discovered was called Mayur – asked Bela: "Monica was famous before this movie became the unexpected hit of the year, but what has life been like for you since *Jigsaw?*"

Bela was looking beautiful with her hair in two cute buns on either side of her head and a white lehenga skirt and crop top fully embroidered with pearls. She looked almost grown-up enough to be cast as an adult lead in a movie.

"I'm overwhelmed with all the support and love I've received," Bela told Mayur. "I was surprised at the movie's success. Credit goes to the Academy," she added. "Without this amazing school – and of course the Dance Starz show that gave me a scholarship – I wouldn't be here."

I clapped and smiled. Bela was so sweet. What a good advertisement she was for the Academy! My mom was such a fan.

Mayur then asked Bela about her experience of working with Om Shankara, the film industry's most famous director. "I learned so much," Bela gushed. "I could totally identify with the character I played. I can't believe I got to work on such a prestigious project so early. Shooting with this amazing director and an

awesome team in locations like Mauritius and Thailand is something I will remember forever. Thank you Om ji and thank you BA."

A massive cheer went up. Miss Takkar was sitting a row in front of me, dabbing tears from her eyes and smiling broadly.

In my happy and emotional state, I'd almost forgotten the reason I had butterflies in my stomach. My band was about to perform the song I'd helped them write, live in front of squillions!

"Before we continue with our ceremony – including the awards for best male actor, best music composer and best director – we have the final act from the Bollywood Academy. Presenting the incredible, the talented... B-Tunes!"

I jumped with excitement. "B-Tunes! B-Tunes!" I screamed in anticipation. I hurriedly sat down again when someone tapped me on the shoulder to tell me I was blocking their view. Seated, I carried on clapping wildly.

Zeeshan, wearing a black leather biker jacket with embellished collars, rushed onto the stage with his guitar. Raktim, smiling and looking fully energized, banged on the drums that had been sitting on one side of the stage. Joya looked like a real pop star with her pretty pink tulle dress that flared out at the waist paired with black leather boots. Her hair was bundled up in a messy bun and she wore sunglasses. What a queen!

Joya sang beautifully and I was glad to see Zeeshan had the audience enthralled when he performed his guitar solo. I looked around and, apart from some of the tables who were too engrossed in food and chat, saw that most of the audience were bopping along or smiling as they watched.

I was overcome with emotion. They were killing it!

Then it hit me.

No one listening knew that I'd had any part to play in it. Not Dilip. Not Miss Takkar. Not the row in front of me. Not the millions of people watching at home in different nations.

Why was I sitting with the audience watching this scene? I should have been on that stage, in the midst of it all, soaking up the praise and adulation! Adrenaline should have been coursing through my veins! Not this heavy feeling in the very pit of my stomach.

I felt happy for B-Tunes but the overarching emotion – and one I was not proud of – was jealousy.

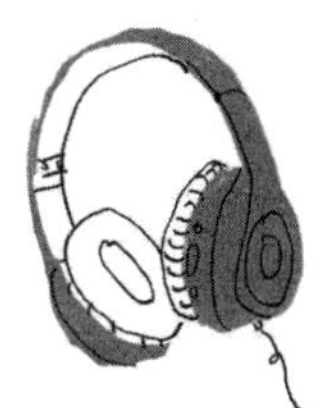

TAKE SEVEN

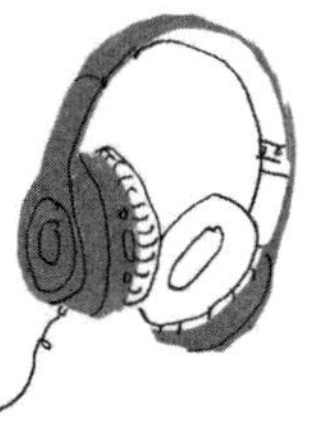

"Ada," said Miss Patel, pointing to the front row.

I had a feeling Miss Patel, who was charged with teaching the Introduction to Film Dialogue module as well as dance, was either going to pick the worst in class or the best.

Ada was the best. She was from Morocco. Her dad owned a string of Bollywood cinema houses there and she loved the movies so much, she was taking private Hindi classes to catch up with the rest of us. Ada's dedication, and the reach of Bollywood, never failed to surprise me.

Ada adjusted her hair clip and flashed a bright smile.

"Yes, miss," she replied sweetly.

"Let's do a scenario," suggested Miss Patel. "Make up your own dialogue – it doesn't matter what. I just want to see emotion in the dialogue delivery. How we say the words is as important as the words themselves."

Ada nodded eagerly. She walked to the front, stood in front of Miss Patel, and reeled off a string of sentences in Hindi. It was weird for us to be talking in Hindi in class. All of our classes were in English, but this module had

to be in Hindi since it was about the dialogue used in Bollywood films.

Ada invented a scenario of a woman going to the hospital to beg for treatment for her elderly father. Her accent might have given her away but every word she spoke contained raw emotion.

"How is Ada not laughing while she's looking at Miss P that way?" I asked Zeeshan who was sitting next to me. He shrugged his shoulders and chuckled.

"I wouldn't be able to. I'm dreading my turn," he whispered back.

The class gave Ada a huge round of applause and she looked pleased as she made her way back to her seat. Now it was her best friend Leena's turn.

"Are we going to have to watch every student demonstrate?" I whispered to Zeeshan.

"Looks like it," he replied.

That was too much for me. I was bored already and could see that there were at least twenty people who would be demonstrating before I was called up. I slipped my hand into my pocket and pulled out my AirPods, removing my scrunchie and shaking out my hair to cover my ears. I kept the volume low but was happy to be hooked up to some mellow music.

Zeeshan's mouth dropped open when he realized what

I was doing. *What do you think you're doing?* he scribbled on his notepad.

Listening to music duh! I scribbled back. *There's 2 whole rows to get through before my turn. I'll be ready for my go.*

I fixed a half-smile on my face to give the impression I was listening to Miss Patel when really I was listening to music, and then I allowed my mind to wander. A few minutes passed. I saw Zeeshan turn toward me but I didn't think much of it.

It was only when he kicked me hard under the table that I turned to look at him. Slowly, I turned toward Miss Patel. She was looking right at me. Or was she looking at my ears? I blushed and quickly dropped my cell phone into my bag which sat under my desk.

"Simi, didn't you hear me? Come down here at once!" she said so loudly the whole school could have heard.

I pretended I was adjusting my hair but quickly pulled the AirPods out of my ears and kept them in my hands. I went and stood in front of Miss Patel, ready to take my turn. I kept my clenched hands by my side.

"I would like you to speak using your hands to convey emotion," she told me.

"Huh?" I asked.

"Open your hands," she commanded.

I put my hands out but wouldn't open my fists.

"Open your hands," she ordered. I had no choice.

A few people gasped while others snickered when they realized what I had done.

"Well, well, well. Listening to music in my class?" Miss Patel kept her gaze on me, piercing me like daggers.

I looked down, ashamed at being caught.

"Let's see what Miss Takkar has to say about this!"

It was excruciatingly embarrassing having to stand at the front on my own as one of the students was sent out to get Miss Takkar. She didn't look too happy when she waltzed in.

"You'll be dealt with according to the rules of the Academy." Miss Takkar cast her eyes across the rest of the students who were all now silent. "You'll have to spend lunch times and break times for two full days doing community service and be thankful we won't confiscate your technology as well!"

If I'd hoped Miss T would soften and give me a lesser punishment after having time to sleep on it, boy was I wrong. She didn't budge and Mrs. Arora, the Principal, approved it too.

A whole two days of not being able to spend break times with my friends was miserable. I was tasked with cleaning and polishing the artificial flowers, leaves and petals in the Smart Garden. It was fun for the first ten minutes or so but the novelty soon wore off.

I was so relieved when the weekend came.

The sounds of birds singing outside my room on Saturday morning seemed sweeter than ever. Kohinoor island was quite small but there were so many birds – including noisy seagulls that always made me feel like I was on vacation.

I turned over and decided to lie in a little longer. It had been a busy and tiring week. Traveling back from Agra on Sunday evening, going straight into class on Monday morning, and then working myself to the bone in the Smart Garden every break time had left no time to rest. I was looking forward to hanging with my friends and jamming with the band again.

Joya was already up and about – I could hear her in the shower. As usual, her side of the room was messier than mine. There were a fair few loom band kits scattered about on the floor and on her desk. Joya had been up making novelty items until late.

I stayed in bed for another twenty minutes, scrolling through my phone. I quickly saved a tune that was in my head on SoundCloud then decided to google my name to see if there were any mentions of me after the OBAs. It was a little disheartening to find nothing: a few general references to the Academy being present and some talk

about the *Jigsaw* gang.

I was interrupted by a call from Mom. I'd been expecting this call for a couple of days but even so, I wasn't ready to face her considering she was still mad at me over my OBAs performance.

"Going on such a big stage and performing soccer tricks of all things! That isn't the sort of recognition we sent you to the Academy for," she'd moaned after the show. "Are you deliberately trying to kill your career before it even starts?"

What would she say this time?

"Simi, I've just seen the email the BA sent two days ago. I ignored it at first because I thought it was another one of their fundraising emails, but I couldn't believe my eyes when I read it. How could you disrespect your teacher by listening to music when she was teaching you about dialogue delivery? Can you imagine Priya doing anything like that?"

I rolled my eyes.

Dad got on the phone too. "I'm really disappointed to be getting these kinds of complaints about you, Simi."

I'd expected Mom to be annoyed, but having Dad tell me off made me feel even worse. What had I done that was so bad? I'd only been listening to music! Tears were welling up in my eyes. I felt bad about upsetting my parents but sorry for myself too.

I dabbed my eyes when Joya came out of the shower in a pretty floral dress with her wet hair wrapped in a towel. She dumped the towel on the bed before hurriedly combing her hair.

"Why are you dressed so early?" I asked, checking the time on the wall clock. It was only 8:45am.

"I'm going to Kohinoor town," she mumbled, her back to me.

"Really?" Students rarely got to go to Kohinoor town. It wasn't a town as such, rather a town square with a council hall, old church, a few basic shops, restaurants and a huge fish market.

"With the boys," she added very quietly.

"Huh? Zee and Raktim?" I sat up.

"Yeah... To celebrate the success of the show last week."

"Oh wow!" I stood up. "How did I miss this? What time are we going?"

"Umm," Joya turned to look at me. "It's just for B-Tunes. I mean, of course you're in B-Tunes, but the B-Tunes that performed at the OBAs."

"Oh..." I tried to keep a neutral expression but my face fell. Not only was I not invited, I had stupidly assumed I would be. How embarrassing.

"But you can't go into town without an adult, right?" I questioned.

"Mr. Joshi is treating us," Joya told me. "We were in his group for the OBAs and after the ceremony, he promised he'd take us out."

Wow. Okay. So Mr. Joshi too. *Gulp*. I felt like I'd been taken off the soccer field to sit on the bench and watch the game from the sidelines.

Joya continued to get ready. She applied some sunscreen as she always did and added a little lip gloss. She then opened the silver jewelry box that sat on her dresser and chose some earrings.

I laid back down again and turned over.

She muttered a quiet "Bye" as she left but I pretended I was asleep.

As soon as she'd gone, I bolted out of bed. I took a very deep breath. I felt a mixture of hurt, anger and self-pity. I needed to break this down bit by bit to make sense of it.

If Mr. Joshi was taking them out to celebrate the success of their performance, of course he wouldn't have invited me, I got that. But why didn't I know about this? Yes, I'd been busy doing community service in the Smart Garden but I'd sat with Zeeshan in the dining hall during the evenings. And I shared a room with Joya

– how long had she known? Not to mention Raktim – usually so efficient and communicative on WhatsApp, he always made sure everybody got all the correct information about everything all the time!

I spent a good half hour playing around with my guitar, thinking things through. Maybe I was overreacting? Maybe I wasn't. All I knew for sure was that I felt excluded and hurt.

You can either sit here and cry, or go out and do something else instead, I told myself.

I scrolled through the BA app on my phone and saw that there were swimming slots available. I booked a session, gathered my belongings as fast as I could and headed out.

As I approached the doors of the Swiminoor – a fully glass building which housed our swimming pool and spa – I saw the one person I didn't want to see. Miss Takkar was unmistakable, despite being in a navy sweatsuit instead of a formal skirt and blazer.

I tried to find a way to dodge her but the path I was walking up led straight to her. The only way to avoid her was to turn back, but that would have been too obvious. She also seemed to want to avoid me. She looked at me and then quickly glanced away. I watched as she stepped left and then right, but found she had nowhere to go except the grass verges on either side of the path.

Suddenly, and most unexpectedly, Mr. Pereira appeared right behind her. “Darling, shall we go for coffee?”

I blushed. Miss Takkar blushed. Mr. Pereira – who had just noticed me – coughed a very fake and nervous cough. I wanted to laugh, but I held it in. I took a few steps and smiled as Miss T approached me.

“Oh hello, Simi!” she said, a little too cheerfully.

“Hello, miss,” I squeaked, keeping my eyes firmly on her. “Hello, sir.”

Mr. Pereira acknowledged me with a simple nod but walked straight past. He didn’t want to stop for a chat and he was definitely pretending that he wasn’t with Miss Takkar.

“Are you well?” she asked me with a tight smile.

“Yes, miss.”

“You did a good job of cleaning up the Smart Garden. I’m sure you won’t make such an error of judgment again.”

“No, miss.”

Miss Takkar continued on her way, as I continued on mine. Gosh, that was awkward!

I decided I wouldn’t make a big deal of the secret I had discovered about her and Mr. Pereira since it would spread like wildfire. If it did, Miss Takkar would know for sure it was me. I was already in enough trouble; revealing facts about Miss T's private life wouldn't help.

I had bigger things to worry about anyway. While I did my laps in the pool, I imagined the conversation I'd have with Zeeshan about why he hadn't mentioned the Kohinoor town lunch plans to me.

The more I thought about it, the bigger the issue became in my head. It turned into such a big deal that when I saw him later that evening at dinner time, I found I couldn't say anything at all. There seemed to be an awkwardness hanging over us and the words just got stuck in my throat.

"Let's go down to the Games Room," suggested Raktim once we'd all eaten.

I considered making an excuse but stopped myself. It seemed silly distancing myself from my friends after having spent lunch breaks and break times alone. I decided to go along.

We all walked down to the Games Room and settled for playing snooker. I wasn't an experienced snooker player but when it came to sports, I had a knack for picking things up quickly. I'm pretty sure it was all about confidence. Perfect Priya always said "I'm really bad at sports" without even trying. Just another one of the

many reasons I found her so annoying.

Joya settled into an armchair and got her laptop out. "You guys play and I'll catch up on my show," she said, logging into Netflix to stream her favorite K-drama.

I braced myself. It was now or never.

"How was the trip to town?" I asked, bending over to cue the ball. I noticed through the corner of my eye that Joya and Raktim exchanged a glance.

The red ball went straight into the pocket, the white ball lining up nicely for me to aim it at the black. "Yes!" I punched the air. Nothing got me out of a bad mood like succeeding in sports. As Mr. Joshi said, winning is addictive.

Zeeshan clapped. "Shot!"

After a brief pause, he ran his fingers through his hair and added: "Yeah, it was nice."

"What did you do?" I asked, trying to sound casual.

"Had lunch with Mr. Joshi," said Zeeshan. "He was cool. He thinks we have the talent to make it in the music business. We just need to work hard now."

"Oh, wow," I commented, forcing a wooden-looking smile. Acting, as it turned out, wasn't my best skill.

"Ouch!" the black ball ricocheted around the table as I tried and failed to get it in the pocket. I passed the cue to Raktim.

"I've always wanted to go to town," I told nobody in particular. "There was a chance to visit last year but I didn't get picked. There are never enough teachers to take us. It's too bad we can't go without the staff."

"Yeah, we wished you could have been there," said Zeeshan. "I guess we have to get used to it though. You're focusing on acting so you'll be off doing different things from us. I can't see you spending so much time in the Noise Zone when you have acting auditions, rehearsals and stuff to get involved with."

I watched as he spoke. He wasn't saying anything false, but he'd accepted it like it didn't matter.

I'd contributed so much to B-Tunes. I'd even helped to create the song for the OBAs that had resulted in the day out they'd just enjoyed so much. I'd never thought I wouldn't be an integral part of the band, and now I wasn't even sure if he still wanted me in it at all.

I didn't dare ask.

I bent down quickly to tie my shoelaces which didn't need tying at all. I just didn't want my best friend and my bandmates to see the tears welling up in my eyes.

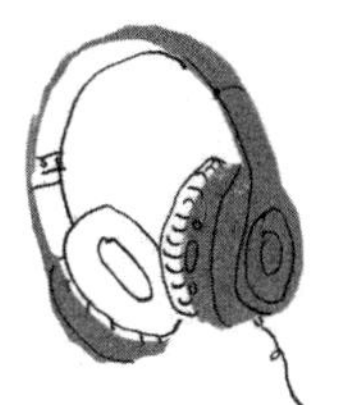

TAKE EIGHT

I cuddled up on the sofa with Gauri as we watched a 1990s Bollywood movie together. This was pretty much all we'd done for the two days I'd been back for the midterm break.

Earlier, I'd heard Mom on the phone, complaining to her agent that she'd been offered a role to play someone's grandmother. Maybe that was why she was a little touchy when we started singing the title track at full volume.

"Uff," she huffed, getting up off the sofa where she was lying down with a face mask and cucumbers on her eyes. She removed them and placed them on a plate. I'd gotten used to finding little plates with shriveled up pieces of cucumber on them.

"Join in, Ma," I giggled.

Gauri got up, perhaps sensing Mom wasn't in the mood. "Simi, I have to prepare lunch," she stated. "We can watch the rest later."

She scurried off to the kitchen while I flicked through the channels, settling for MTV as background noise. I picked up the latest copy of the *Tollywood Express* and found an interesting article about how Telugu movies

were catching up with Bollywood.

Mom tutted as she walked past. "Are you reading magazines or watching TV? You can't do both."

"Why'd you send me all the way to Mumbai?" I asked her. "Telugu movies are doing almost as well as Hindi movies, no? See this," I held up the magazine. "It says they're making a lot of money at the box office."

Mom had stopped by the gold leaf mirror that hung over a metallic sideboard in the living room to peel off her face mask.

"Not the same if you want international glory," she informed me before continuing with her beauty regime.

"I don't remember saying I want international glory," I said. "Maybe you want it for me?"

Mom put down her tools and almost drilled a hole through me with her stare. Perhaps I'd gone too far. The confusion I was feeling about my future career as an actor and the tension I was feeling over B-Tunes were affecting me, obviously.

"That was a joke, Mom," I said. I really didn't want to create an atmosphere here too. "But seriously, are the movies in South India not as good, if not better, than Bollywood?"

Mom shook her head. "No."

"Why not?"

"Well, for one thing, India will always have more Hindi speaking people than Telugu speakers. Hindi is our national language while Telugu is regional."

"Fair point," I conceded.

"Secondly," said Mom, plucking out rogue eyebrow hairs with a pair of tweezers, "globally, Bollywood will always be king. Way more people around the world watch Bollywood than Tollywood."

I nodded.

"And finally," she concluded, "Bollywood music is way better than the music in Telugu movies – you should know that."

"Yes! You're right, Mom," I said, standing up. "I was thinking the other day, why did I grow up wanting to watch Bollywood over Telugu movies? Music's a big part of that. The songs are the soul of Bollywood. I'm gonna discuss it with Dad later," I added excitedly. "I'm off to the studio – I have a really good tune in my head for a sad song."

Mom tutted. "One of these days, I'm going to turn that studio of yours into a library or something useful."

"Empty threats," I shouted back at her as I bounded up the stairs. The best thing about coming home was being able to use my studio, without having to book it or be kicked out after an hour.

I got to work quickly; I didn't want to forget what was in my head. I picked up my phone first and recorded the sound of myself humming the tune to keep it firmly in mind. I had mapped out the instrumental lines for the opening of the song but couldn't decide on the chorus. I then logged onto my computer and got to work. I'd only been up there for an hour when Mom called me back down again.

"Yeah, Mom?"

I was surprised to see her standing at the bottom of the stairs in sportswear, her hair up in a bun.

"Have you joined a gym?" I asked.

"Yes. I'm going to a Pilates class," she told me. "It helps to strengthen and tone, boosts blood circulation and youthfulness. I must be in the best possible condition for my audition on Friday."

She waited by the door for our driver, Rajiv, to arrive.

"How long will you be gone?" I asked. "Can we go into town after lunch, get some ice cream or watch a movie?"

"Sorry, Simi," she said, looking a little downbeat. "After the gym, I'm having a facial to rejuvenate my skin and get rid of some of these blackheads." She pointed to what looked like regular mom skin to me. "Have lunch with Gauri."

I smiled a half-smile and caught Gauri looking at me

from the kitchen door. She could always guess at what I was feeling, perhaps better than Mom could.

Once Mom had left, I went back to the studio but I wasn't in the mood anymore. I was used to Mom being too preoccupied for me most of the time, but it hadn't bothered me during the summer vacation when I'd been busy with B-Tunes, either Facetiming the guys or creating new songs. I was still feeling bruised by my bandmates' secret trip to Kohinoor town. And something else was bothering me too.

Right after the snooker game, I had quit the B-Tunes 4 Life Whatsapp group. I'd felt so upset at Zeeshan's comments about me going on "a different path," I didn't think I should be part of it anymore. I didn't feel like I was wanted.

I wondered if they'd invite me to re-join. Had they messaged me to check on me or invite me back in?

Nope. Nothing.

Dad, wot time r u home? I typed. *Can we go out?*

Sorry, Simi darl, he replied. *I'm still in makeup. We have a whole scene to finish. So many issues today. I won't be home until after dark.*

No probs, I replied with a sad-face emoji followed by a heart.

I switched off my phone.

"Mom and Dad busy?" asked Gauri as she popped her head around the door. I nodded as I sank into the beanbag that sat under the window.

"Show me," said Gauri, wiping her hands on a dish towel. She removed her sandals and walked toward me.

"Huh?"

"Show me how to make music," she told me. "I want to learn."

I smiled. I knew she was only saying it to make me happy but it was working. Spending time in the studio was my absolute favorite thing to do. But I also craved company. It was hard being an only child and harder still being the daughter of parents who were busy all the time.

We had lunch in the studio – a strict no-no according to Mom. And we had a blast. Trying to make music with her made me realize that some people really are tone deaf! I tried to show her how to mix a couple of tunes – DJ Dan ones of course – and it was hilarious to see her get so confused over all the knobs and the equipment. It was only when Mom came back at 4pm that Gauri rushed back into the kitchen to put the tea on.

"Simi!"

I trudged back downstairs. Mom had her biggest black sunglasses on, even though she was indoors, and stood there with her hands covering both sides of her face.

"You okay?" I asked, stepping toward her. She turned her back to me.

"Where's that cooling coconut balm I bought a few weeks back? The green pot? My skin's a little sensitive right now."

I remembered seeing it in the mirror cabinet and ran to the bathroom to get it. Mom took it while looking the other way, before disappearing into her room. There was no chance she was going to take me out now, I knew that for sure.

"Can you tell Mom I'm going to see Jai?" I told Gauri as I popped my phone into my cross-body bag. "She probably won't notice but..."

I didn't finish the sentence.

I walked out then charged down our street, taking a shortcut through our local park to Jai's house. Even though he was only ten minutes away, the road he lived on was nothing like ours. The houses were a lot smaller and more modest, but it always felt more alive. The noise, the people and the friendly chaos were welcoming.

As I approached Jai's house, I saw him playing cricket in the road with his little brother, Viraj. I ran toward them.

"Hey, Simi!" he said, his face lighting up. "Come,

play!"

I didn't need a second invitation. We took it in turns to bat and bowl. The local community had recently campaigned to stop cars coming down this road and the kids were obviously loving it.

"Jai! Viraj!"

We turned and saw Jai's mom standing in the doorway with a plate of food. She always wore simple cotton sarees with bright, pretty patterns. Today, she was wearing a saree with a gray base and a beautiful bird print with vibrant pinks and greens.

Jai looked at me. "Let's go inside, Simi, and have some tea."

Why would I say no? It looked delicious!

"Simi didi, give me a piggyback please," urged Viraj. His little round face with missing teeth was so cute, I couldn't say no to him either – particularly when he addressed me as "older sister" so respectfully. I crouched down to let him climb up on my back and the three of us made our way inside.

"Namaste, Auntie Ji," I greeted Jai's mom.

"Namaste, Simi," she said. "You should have told me you were coming! I would have prepared something special."

She ran around a little, folding the throw that had

been chucked onto the sofa and plumping up some cushions.

"It's fine, auntie. I'm happy with whatever you have. I can help you." I got up to move to the kitchen.

"Absolutely not!" she said. "You're our guest. How is your dad?"

"He's fine," I told her. "Busy as ever."

Jai and I giggled. He'd told me his mom was a big Shyam Prasad fan.

Jai's mom didn't have a maid and did all the cooking, cleaning and housework herself. She dashed off and came back in from the kitchen with steaming masala chai – I could smell the cardamoms – plus a plate of jalebis and some aloo tikki.

"Yum!" I squealed. Viraj and I both rushed at it at once. "I love jalebis," I said, enjoying the deliciously crunchy, sticky sweet snack.

"I can see that," chuckled Jai. He was wearing the Nike T-shirt I'd bought him for his birthday. I was glad he liked it.

Viraj dug into the spicy potato cakes while Jai's mom asked me questions about home, the Academy and life in general. She always took an interest in me. As I sipped my tea, I thought about how weird it was that Jai and I had such similar interests but our moms couldn't have

been more different.

"I'll walk you back," said Jai when we were done. I said bye to auntie and gave little Viraj a big hug, promising to bring him candy next time.

"It's so cool being your friend," I told Jai as we made our way back to mine. The sun was setting now. The birds were still happily chirping away and there was that lovely smell of summer hanging in the air.

"Yeah? How?" he asked with a smile. "You're the daughter of the superstar! You're the one studying at the Academy on your way to becoming a brilliant Bollywood star! I'm glad to be *your* friend."

I kept my head down and walked a few steps in silence.

"All those things aren't that important," I said eventually. "It's not that simple."

Jai looked confused so I took a deep breath and told him everything that had happened at school. How I wasn't sure if B-Tunes were kicking me out or ghosting me or whether it was all in my head. How I wasn't sure I was cut out for a career as an actor or if I even wanted one.

As we stood at a crossroads, waiting for cars to pass so we could get to the other side, I told him of the crossroads I found myself at in life.

TAKE EIGHT

"But I don't get it," remarked Jai. We walked to the other side of the road and sat down on a bench in the park that separated my world from Jai's. "You've always talked about wanting to be an actor."

I sighed. "Well, yeah – maybe because that's what everyone told me I wanted. But did I ever dream it for myself?"

"So you don't want to act anymore?" he looked shocked. "What changed?"

"I can't seem to get excited about it," I told Jai. "I find it weird pretending to be somebody else."

He chuckled at that, helping himself to the piece of sugar-free strawberry gum I offered.

"But isn't that exactly what acting is?" he laughed. "So why are you at a stage school then?"

I shrugged my shoulders. "Bollywood Academy isn't just acting, is it? There are other jobs I could do."

"Well, yeah, you're right. You could be a film director or a producer," he suggested.

"Or a music composer," I offered.

Jai's eyes lit up. He stood. "Yes! You're a musical genius!" he laughed. "Why not? Why didn't we think of that before?"

I was so glad to see him lending his support. But I was still uncertain about my options.

Jai and I took a few goofy selfies in the park and I promised to WhatsApp them over to him later. When I got home, I chose one for my profile picture.

Suddenly, WhatsApp wasn't such a sad place anymore.

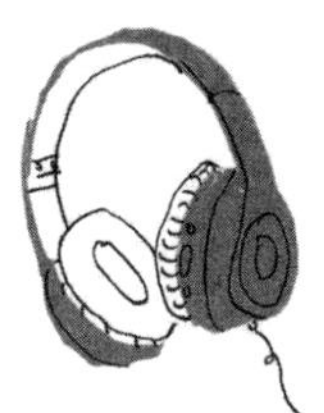

TAKE NINE

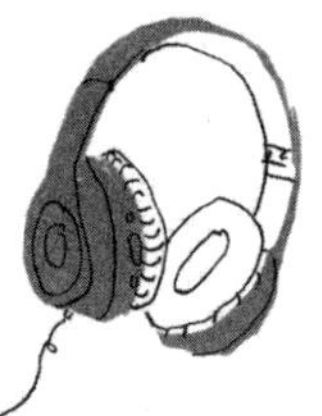

Mom was in a flap – again. I could hear her having a go at Gauri and Kanta, our cleaning lady, so I jumped out of bed and ran downstairs. I soon found out that Mom's hair and makeup lady had let her down so she was trying to find somebody else who could step in at a moment's notice.

"I have a very important audition today," she said in tense tones to somebody on the other end of the line. She was waving around a piece of paper in her hand with the lines she had to learn. Gauri was frantically scrolling through her phone, no doubt trying to find a replacement.

I could imagine why Mom was so stressed. It had been months since she'd been called up for any jobs. And I think she had lost her agent too. At least I hadn't seen or heard anything about the agent since Mom had screamed at her on the phone, accusing her of doing nothing to get her jobs.

"I need you immediately," Mom demanded. "I have to leave in two hours. I have no time to waste." The desperation was real. "I will pay you twice the rate! Will

you *now* do the job?"

I was relieved when the person on the other end agreed. Kanta looked happy too. She quickly grabbed her mop and broom and decided to go upstairs to start sweeping the marble tiles on the landing. Everybody wanted to stay out of Mom's way when she was this stressed.

Mom was wearing a Punjabi suit – a fitted tunic with sharara trousers which were tight on the thigh and then flared out at the ankle. She had heels on but didn't like them so threw them off and ordered Gauri to go and get her sandals from upstairs.

"What's the gig, Mom?" I asked, biting into a custard cream cookie I'd stolen from the kitchen pantry.

"Not too much sugar, Simi," Mom scolded. "It will make you hyper! It's breakfast time. Eat fruit – at least that's natural sugar. Your auntie was telling me how much fruit Priya has every day. No wonder her skin is so glowing and rosy."

Of course Perfect Priya started her perfect day with the perfect breakfast.

Mom squeezed her feet into the sandals Gauri passed to her. They looked hideously uncomfortable. I would never bother – sneakers were so much cooler and more comfy. She then tried to balance herself in front of the hallway mirror again.

"What did you ask me, Simi?"

"What's the audition for?"

"To be on the judging panel of a TV talent show – Talented Tots," said Mom.

"Oh, that contest for little kids?"

She nodded. "It's like Dance Starz but general talent, not just dance."

"Oh wow, that's cool."

"I hope I get it. These shows are so popular. Once you get onto one, you'll get onto all of them and become a household name."

I prayed she would get it. It might help with her mood swings as well as her confidence. I'd heard her on the phone to one of her friends the other day complaining about people calling her Mrs. Shyam Prasad. "I'm more than just his wife," she'd ranted.

"How come Dad gets jobs so easily?" I asked, prompted by the memory.

Mom looked at me through the mirror she was using to adjust the sequined dupatta that completed her outfit. "Perhaps because he's a man and it doesn't matter how old he is?"

"Huh? Is that what you think?"

She turned to me as our doorbell rang and the

makeup artist rushed in, wheeling a bag behind her. "I don't *think* – I *know*! It's obvious. All the heroes in our movies either down here or in Bollywood, they can be fifty plus but the actresses are never older than thirty! Name me one movie where that's not the case."

She led the lady through to the living room.

I thought about what Mom had said. She was right. I mean, of course Dad got jobs because of who he was and his talent, but I couldn't think of a single movie where a female actor in a lead part was older than, say, thirty-five? Most of them looked like they were in their mid-to-late twenties.

And like Mom said, so many male actors carried on playing leading roles until they were gray. I wondered how and why this was happening and how it was allowed to carry on. It seemed as though Mom was battling two things: being an older woman in an industry that gave more opportunities to men *and* to younger people. No wonder she was always on edge.

But ever since I could remember, she had been fighting the fight as best she could. And this usually meant that I had to compete with her ambition to get some attention – which is why I was so glad when she told me the following morning that she'd be spending the whole day with me. I was fully expecting something to come up and Mom to ditch me for it, but that didn't happen.

After brunch, Mom drove me to the Film Nagar Dessert Parlor – the best ice cream shop for miles around. I dipped my spoon into my sundae glass that was piled high with different-flavored scoops of ice cream and sprinkles. *Yum.* I closed my eyes so I could savor it.

"I miss this when I'm at the Academy," I told Mom, chocolate sauce dripping down one side of my mouth. Mom passed me a handkerchief. "We're not even allowed to go into Kohinoor town," I moaned.

I eyed Mom's small bowl while I continued eating mine. She was having a single scoop of plain kulfi ice cream with a sprig of mint. It looked nice but there was hardly anything to it.

"Do you want some of mine, Mom?"

"No, thank you, darling," she said as she took tiny little pieces of her kulfi and allowed them to melt in her mouth. "I heard sugar breaks down collagen and makes your skin saggy and old." She patted the sides of her face, as though to check it wasn't happening right now.

"Your face looks perfectly fine to me," I laughed, taking another delicious mouthful. "This is too good. Discipline is for adults."

Mom's next nibble was interrupted by her cell phone.

"Oh, it's the production company!" she said. She stood up and then sat down again. She looked anxious as she accepted the call.

I crossed my fingers under the table as I watched her face. A few tense minutes passed.

"To whom?" she said finally, her voice haughty and cold. "Oh, I see – Rahi Chandrega. The 20-year-old Miss India contestant who didn't even make the final 40 at the Miss World finals."

Mom put her handset down in a huff. She didn't even say goodbye to whoever was on the phone. The disappointment was written all over her face.

"Don't worry, Mom," I said. I pushed my empty dish away and wiped my mouth. "Talented Tots isn't the best reality show anyway."

Mom prodded the remaining half of her kulfi but didn't eat it. It melted away on her plate until all that was left was a watery puddle.

*

Mom looked downbeat for the next couple of days.

I tried to cheer her up by watching a couple of episodes of a new Netflix series but it seemed like the audition rejection had really knocked the wind out of her. She had stopped wearing makeup. Her hair was scraped back into a low ponytail and she spent most of the day lying down with her eyes closed or staring blankly at the TV.

"I'm bored, Mom," I told her, squeezing myself into a few inches of space next to her on the sofa and taking a corner of the blanket.

I logged onto an online band meeting to discover that Joya, Raktim and Zeeshan were already there but in a separate virtual room. I checked my phone to see if I'd missed the invitation. Nope. I quickly logged off and pulled the blanket up higher toward my chin.

It was even weirder because it was Zeeshan's birthday. I'd sent him a "*Hugratulations on becoming a teenager!*" message first thing in the morning. He'd sent me a "*Thank u, Simi*" reply followed by a heart emoji and a link to his new Instagram account with the handle @Mr.ZeeMan but no mention of the online meeting.

Maybe if I hadn't quit the B-Tunes 4 Life group they would have asked me? Did they think I'd left the group because I didn't want to be in the band anymore?

I felt anxious and on edge. I tried to calm myself down by sighing a big, deep, heavy and noisy sigh.

"Why don't you go with your dad?" said Mom, her face mostly hidden by the other end of the blanket.

"Go where?"

"He has an interview with that chat show host – I forget his name."

"Balay Surma?"

"No, the other one."

"Rajan Bal?"

"Yes, that's right."

I stood up. "No way?!"

Rajan Bal was amazing. He'd interviewed so many big names over the years. There would be nothing better to do on a dull day like today than visit his studio.

"Or you can go and visit Priya? Rajiv can take you," she suggested.

"I'm going with Dad," I stated, leaving Mom no chance to mention Perfect Priya again.

I found Dad on the phone in his office. He stretched his arms out wide, inviting me in for a hug. I scribbled on a notepad on the big executive desk. Dad's office was decked out in mahogany furniture and dark green leather.

Can I go to the TV studio with you? I wrote.

Dad continued his conversation – he was talking money so I gathered he was negotiating the rate for his next job. But he nodded.

Be ready at 11, he wrote back.

I smiled and gave him a thumbs up before dashing off to get dressed. This was the hard part. I couldn't wear a sweatsuit to a TV studio – you never knew who you'd meet there. I opted for light blue skinny jeans and a cropped T-shirt with an image of a set of headphones. Dad had bought it for me from an airport a few months back as he'd said it reminded him of me.

"Maybe I could give Perfect Priya some competition," I giggled to myself as I completed my look with a silver necklace my Naani had given me.

I enjoyed the 15-minute car journey to the Tinsel Film Studios mainly because I had time to chat to Dad. "The TV show you're judging, when does it finish?"

"Just two more episodes," he replied. "Some of the acts are incredible. It's going to be an amazing show."

"And then what?"

"I'm starting a TV series for Amazon Prime. A serious acting job for a change," he laughed. "A thriller – and it's going to be in a mix of Hindi and English. That's what the international audiences want these days."

"Oh!" I was impressed. I couldn't recall a time when Dad didn't have at least two different projects on the go.

It made me think of Mom. I felt guilty for leaving her at home.

"I wish Mom had more work," I said. "I think she

wants to feel more useful."

"Yes, she does." Dad looked pained. It was obvious he felt for her. "But dozens of people audition for the roles your Mom goes for. It's natural she can't get all of them."

"But is it natural she can't get any of them?" I replied. He didn't seem to have an answer for that.

Dad ruffled my hair as we got out of the car – to my horror, of course. I'd spent ten minutes neatly parting it and flicking out the sides. I got my phone out and put it in selfie mode to check the damage.

As we walked to the entrance, we were greeted by a studio runner who took us to the desk to sign in and then off to the makeup room where Dad had a little powder applied to remove any shine from his face.

"Now to the Green Room," said the runner, showing us the way. I'd been to enough studios in my life to know that this was the space where you waited before going live on air. This Green Room, though, was a pretty spectacular one. Tinsel Film Studios had gone to town with the green theme. Richly upholstered sofas with plush cushions in various emerald tones sat in one corner along with a thick-pile green rug.

There was a big-screen TV right in front of the sofas for guests to watch what was happening in the studio as the show was live on air. A library of books stood tall in the other corner although I doubted anybody would be there long enough to even choose a book, let alone read one. I don't know if it was the reflections off the green items in the room but it seemed as though the books had a greenish tinge to them too.

My favorite item, by far, was the green piano with the green velvet stool.

"Ooh, look at that, Dad!" It was so shiny and pristine with ornate gold writing all the way around in what I thought might have been Mandarin. I'd never seen a green piano before. I was itching to go and play it but of course it was there for aesthetic purposes only.

The chat show host, Rajan Bal, burst in a few moments later and greeted Dad warmly.

"This is my little monkey," Dad told him.

"Ah, beautiful girl!" he remarked.

"She studies at the Bollywood Academy," added Dad.

"Ooh, lucky for her! I saw some of the students perform at the Awards thingy last month. Were you on stage?" he asked me.

I looked at Dad, who chuckled. "Yes – she was the one playing soccer."

I blushed.

"That was *you!*" Rajan Bal put out the palm of his hand. "I need your autograph," he joked. "You were

amazing!"

I wasn't sure whether he was just being polite but I thought it was cool that he remembered me.

The door handle turned again and I literally thought I was going to faint when in walked Mirza Choudhary. He was probably *the* most famous music composer in the history of Bollywood. Of course, that was up for debate but I'd had lots of conversations about how he was for sure one of the Greatest Of All Time if not *the* GOAT.

He looked a lot older than the images and videos I had seen, but I guess it had been twenty years since the peak of his fame. *Was it actually him?*

Mirza Choudhary was more famous than Dad for sure, so I wasn't surprised when Dad got up and walked over to greet him. This didn't usually happen in Film Nagar. Most people came over to Shyam Prasad.

"Mirza sahib," my dad beamed, extending his hand. Mirza Choudhary was wearing a very simple white cotton kurta and linen trousers. He really looked like the artistic type. His shoulder-length hair in black and white tones completed the look. "What an honor to meet you. I've always been a big fan of your work," Dad gushed.

I think Mirza Choudhary recognized Dad because he asked what he was working on next. Of course, Dad mentioned the Hindi Amazon Prime series rather than his Telugu ventures.

"Oh, interesting," Mirza said. "I look forward to seeing it."

They shook hands again and shortly after, a studio runner came in to tell Dad it was time for his interview.

"You can wait here, Simi. Is that okay?"

I nodded. Was I actually going to be alone with Mirza Choudhary? What would I say? My heart started beating really fast but my mind went blank the more I tried to think about talking points.

Dad looked at me then put his hand on my back.

"Mirza sahib, Simi is a natural when it comes to music. She listens, she plays... Test her."

Gulp. I couldn't believe he was putting me on the spot like that!

"Oh, is that so?" the music maestro laughed. He looked really friendly, just how I imagined him. "So, young lady – Simi, is it?"

"Yes," I smiled nervously, biting my lip.

"You have an interest in music?"

"Yes, sir. Very much."

"You play anything?"

"Piano, guitar. A little violin too."

I didn't know whether to look at him or to watch Dad, who I could see on the big screen now. He looked

comfortable chatting to Rajan Bal about his upcoming projects.

"Are you studying music?"

I shook my head. "Not really. I'm at the Bollywood Academy on Kohinoor Island so I'm learning a bit of everything."

"Ah, I was at the OBAs and some of the kids from your school were there," he said.

What? Was he? I didn't see him but then again, how would I have spotted him amongst those thousands of people?

"There was a band there from your Academy. Promising. I liked the song. *Dil se...dil se...* Very catchy."

I suddenly forgot how famous he was and my nervousness at speaking to him. Without planning to, I blurted it out.

"That was my band, sir! And the song was partly mine – as in, I helped compose the melody but the lyrics were Raktim's. He's a friend who's in the band."

"Oh, how nice!" Mirza commented. "So you're the melody queen then, hey? That's what I like to hear. It all starts with the melody."

Melody Queen. I liked that!

"But you weren't there, were you?" Mirza asked me. "I don't remember seeing you on stage."

I felt too embarrassed to tell him that I was the one playing soccer, I don't know why.

"No, sir, I wasn't with the band."

"Well, if you like music, why don't you and your dad come along to the soundtrack release of my new Telugu movie, *My Appa?*"

"You work in Tollywood movies now, sir?"

"Hmm, not really – it was a favor for a friend. But I enjoyed it," he revealed. "That's why I'm here today, to promote the music and the movie."

Mirza began texting somebody to ask them to invite Dad to the event.

"Done!" he said, pressing send. "It will be a pleasure to see you there."

Dad was still on air so I needed to find a topic to talk about.

"Do you remember when you used to record songs with full, live orchestras, uncle?"

"Oh yes – how could I forget?" Mirza smiled as he reminisced. "I still do use live orchestras but they are much scaled down now," he explained. "Even though it's difficult and more expensive, it's a really rewarding way of working. It creates a unique team experience. Can you believe that so-called music composers think they can create new tunes just through computers and sampling?"

He chuckled, almost to himself. I could see this was something that he thought about a lot.

"I could, if I wanted to, pretty much work alone these days but you can't create totally original songs unless you work with real instruments," he continued. "Sampling and all that is great, but the pieces of ready-made music are available to everyone so your work will never be truly original. It all starts to sound a bit...samey."

He stopped to think for a moment and then chuckled. "I blame the DJs, but that's just between you and me." He smiled at me.

I definitely shared his love for live music and live orchestras but I wasn't going to mention how much I depended on samples and loops for my own music!

"What do you remember about the old days, sir?" I asked.

His eyes smiled as he looked into the distance, as though fetching memories from a corner of this beautiful room. "The way we worked was different," he began. "When I started out, arrangers had a key role in deciding what instruments to use. They would then go on to notate the music."

"To create a written score?" I asked.

"Yes, Simi. Exactly."

"And who chose the singers?"

"I did," he told me. "Sometimes in discussion with the film director. In those days, many singers were partnered with male and female actors for the duration of that actor's career. The voices needed to match, and audiences kind of expected that a certain star would have a certain playback singer."

I remembered my Dad talking to me about this once. It was fascinating.

"As a composer, my main job was to get the melody right," Mirza continued, smiling at me as he spoke. "I would then sit with the lyricist and arranger to finalize the orchestration and the harmonies. We took our time...and paid attention to every detail. Nowadays, there seems to be such a shortage of time. Everybody is rushing."

I was mesmerized by the way Mirza sahib was talking so fondly and lovingly about how he used to create music. I could tell it meant so much more to him than just work.

"We'd have as many as thirty violinists alone in the recording sessions!" he told me. "Now, some composers hire five and multitrack instead. I guess it makes financial and practical sense," he conceded.

At that point, Dad walked back in.

"Oh, does that mean it's your turn to go on now?"

I asked Mirza, sad that the chat had come to an end already.

"Yes, my dear," he smiled. "Your smart daughter took me on a trip down Memory Lane," Mirza told Dad. "I'm sending you an invitation to an event this Saturday, Shyam. Make sure you bring Simi – she will enjoy it."

"You two seem to have hit it off," Dad said as we made our way out of the studio. "He's a legend of Bollywood, you know."

"You think I don't know that?" I chuckled. "Please, Dad, please tell me you'll take me to the event he mentioned!"

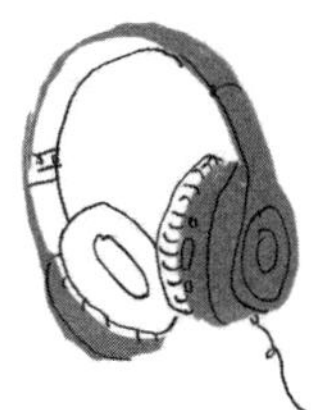

TAKE TEN

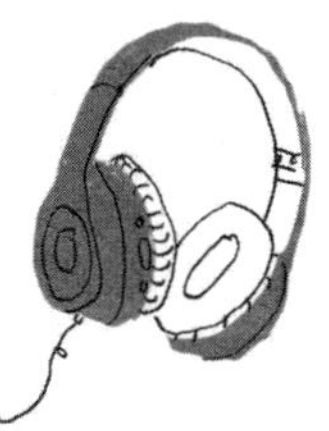

Later that evening, a bunch of flowers with an invitation card addressed to Dad and me landed on our veranda.

"Wow, they're beautiful!" I gushed, taking a deep whiff of the pink and white roses.

I ran inside with them to show Mom. She looked a little bit brighter. She was sitting doing yoga but was still makeup free. I told her all about the chance meeting with Mirza uncle and how he had invited us to the soundtrack launch. She looked pleased.

"Do you want to come, Mom?" I asked, reading the card. "It's at the Film Nagar Cultural Center on Saturday."

She declined with a shake of her head before closing her eyes again to meditate or do whatever else she was doing.

I took my phone and clicked on WhatsApp. I started typing a message to Zeeshan but then stopped. Instead, I decided to check out his new IG account and saw that he'd posted photographs from B-Tunes' day out in Kohinoor town – the day I wasn't invited.

So insensitive, I thought to myself. Why couldn't they

share it privately?

I decided against messaging him but I really wanted to share my experience with somebody who would understand and be happy for me, so I ran off to tell Gauri all about my afternoon. I was pleased she showed so much interest. She knew all of Mirza Choudhary's hit songs. We had a slice of cake while playing a game where one of us hummed a Mirza tune and the other person had to guess the song and the movie. I won, of course!

I still didn't know everything about him, so I decided to go and research him a little more. iPad in hand, I googled his name and clicked on one of the pages where there was an article headlined: "The top 10 Bollywood music composers of all time." Mirza was listed at number four which was incredible for an industry spanning more than a hundred years! I scrolled up to the top and read through the list.

Then it dawned on me.

Not one of the people on the list was female. Not one.

I searched up other similar lists – "Bollywood's Top 25 composers," "Top 50 composers" – and found one female name at best. I was stunned.

Maybe this was how I could break the ice with Zeeshan without sharing too much personal stuff about what either of us was doing?

Did u know that barely 1-2% of Bollywood music composers have been female? I texted him. Zeeshan knew so much about Bollywood music, but I was sure he'd be as shocked as I was. I sent him links to all the articles I'd found.

It took a good few hours for his reply to land. *Yeah... How come u didn't know this?* he said, followed by laughing emojis.

I didn't like his response. Did he not care at all? I decided I wouldn't text him back and now I certainly wasn't going to tell him about my meeting with Mirza Choudhary.

*

The next few days passed in a blur and soon it was the big day.

The sun was setting when I laid excited eyes on the Film Nagar Cultural Center, admiring its pink and white facade. The building was shaped like a semi-circle and had expansive, very neatly maintained grounds. I could see little groups of people standing around outside the main entrance being served drinks and nibbles.

Dad – stylishly dressed in a gray Nehru jacket – complemented me with my gray dress with silver beading

on the waistband. As we made our way to the reception area, I saw that Mirza Choudhary had opted to stand out a little more with a bright red, raw silk kurta top and white trousers. He looked so trendy with his hair pulled back into a low ponytail.

I helped myself to a mini pizza bite when the server came around and Dad took a salmon pakora. Mirza uncle raised his hand and smiled when he caught sight of us. We walked over to him as the paparazzi snapped away.

“So glad you could make it. I insist on a red-carpet shot, Shyam,” he said.

“Yes, why not?” Dad laughed. I took my phone out of my black cross-body bag, ready to take photos of my father with the music legend. They stood against a white backdrop – which I’d learned at school was a step and repeat banner. It had the words *My Appa* repeated across it along with the logos of various companies who were no doubt sponsors.

They posed for a couple of photos when Mirza uncle suddenly stopped. “How are we having pics taken without the Melody Queen herself?”

I raised a hand to my mouth. I couldn’t believe he was calling me that in public! I loved it! I blushed as he came over to get me. He linked his arm in mine and positioned me in between him and Dad. I quickly fixed my hair so it wasn't sitting messily on my shoulders and flashed a wide grin.

"Is this Shyam's daughter?" one of the photographers asked Mirza.

"Yes, indeed. Watch out for her. She's going to be a big star one day," he smiled.

"Following in Shyam's footsteps with a career in Tollywood?" came a voice from the small crowd.

My heart was beating fast. I wasn't used to being in the spotlight like this. I looked up at Dad and smiled as we made our way inside to one of the larger halls where a soothing melody from the movie soundtrack was playing. I'd enjoyed that little bit of attention but it was now showtime.

We took our seats and I listened with interest to the introductory speeches where the *My Appa* filmmakers took to the stage and thanked the guests for attending. They then showered praise on Mirza Choudhary for creating such "haunting and memorable" tunes that would be sure-fire hits. I was trying to take photos but adult heads in the rows in front of us were getting in the way so I gave up.

Next, the lead actors from *My Appa* appeared on stage to say how much they enjoyed working on the movie

while the photographers fought to get the best shots.

"Who are these actors, Dad?" I didn't recognize any of them.

Dad gave me an open-mouthed, incredulous look. "I need to educate you, young lady," he whispered. "Too much time in Bollywood I feel!"

Maybe he was right. I was out of touch with Tollywood movies. I decided I'd do some research when I got home.

Mirza then took the microphone and told us how proud he was to have composed the score for his first-ever Telugu film. "Movies from the South of India are quickly catching up with Bollywood in terms of popularity and box office earnings," he smiled. "There is room for regional movies on the international stage, especially with the rise of streaming channels where language is no longer a barrier."

The crowd loved that. Cheers erupted.

"Now, I have a surprise for you all," he announced when the crowd had quieted down a little.

I straightened up, craning my neck and wondering what it would be.

"An idea that was sparked by a chance conversation with a special young lady," he added.

Dad and I looked quizzically at each other, unsure of

what he meant.

Mirza Choudhary walked off stage, the lights dimmed, and the heavy, luxury velvet curtains slowly parted.

I gasped at what I witnessed next. It was the most fantastic sight: a full orchestra complete with conductor! The young lady he had mentioned – was that me? This is what we had been talking about! I felt a little overwhelmed.

There were rows upon rows of violinists, sitar players, tabla players and flautists. A male and female playback singer took to the microphones and one of the flautists started playing. The graceful notes wafted around the room. I didn't know of any instrument so simple yet so powerful in the effect it could have on a listener.

But it was the violinists who made my eyes well up. The vibrations from the stringed instruments in tandem with each other created a well of emotion in the room. There was a reason all the sad songs in Bollywood movies featured violins. It was soul-stirring.

The hairs on my arms were standing up and the audience was completely silent. The notes felt so real, like you could almost reach out and touch them. The music seemed to be dancing around the hall with us in some kind of physical form.

The audience was spellbound. I was fixated. Dad had tears in his eyes. It was the most beautiful thing I'd seen in my whole life and confirmed what I already knew.

There was nothing I loved more than music.

TAKE ELEVEN

I ran down the corridor, wondering why Mr. Pereira had summoned me to his office. Was I in trouble? Outside his door, I wiped my face with the corner of my school cardigan to make sure I didn't look sweaty. I cleared my throat and gently tapped on the door.

"Enter," came a voice.

I walked in to see Mr. Pereira looking at his laptop screen and scribbling on a notepad at the same time.

"Ah, just the person I wanted to see," he said.

I tried to get the image of him and Miss Takkar at the swimming pool out of my mind. I hoped this wasn't the reason I was there today.

"So, Miss Takkar should be doing this but she's busy with a group of students," he began.

I nodded, feeling a bit anxious.

"We've been approached by a production house seeking a girl aged 11-13 for a movie role."

"Oh," I said, feeling immediately relieved.

"They'd like the girl's actual mother to play the role of her mother in the movie," he elaborated. "It was brought to my attention that your mom is an ex-actor so that

would potentially work very well."

I was sure Mom wouldn't enjoy being called an ex-actor. And I had no idea why they wanted a real-life mother-daughter duo – Mom and I didn't even look that similar. I didn't feel that enthusiastic about this but I knew it was a great opportunity for Mom.

"I'll do it," I said.

"Excellent," replied Mr. Pereira. "I'll be in touch with your mother to let her know I've spoken to you. We can take it from there. The audition is at a studio in Mumbai – to be confirmed."

"Sure, sir."

I shut the door quietly behind me and scooted all the way to the cafeteria where I found Joya, Raktim and Zeeshan digging into paneer pizzas. I dashed to the counter to grab my slice plus my daily dose of vitamins in the form of salad, and took a seat at their table.

Joya smiled at me, moving her chair to make space for me.

"Hey, dost," said Raktim. "How are you? We don't see you at the Noise Zone anymore. What's happening with you? Anything exciting?"

Hmm. I wanted to tell him that they didn't see me at the studio because they didn't invite me, but I decided not to.

"I might have an audition coming up," I told them, beaming widely. I think I was trying to show off. I quickly explained the role to them.

"Sounds fab!" said Raktim.

"I can't believe you and your mom might work together – how cool!" said Joya.

Zeeshan was too busy eating to comment. He just nodded at the news. Did he even care about what I was doing?

"If you get the part and become famous," he said eventually, "make sure you put in a good word for me."

I didn't comment. Why did he make everything about himself? It would have been nice if he'd said something even vaguely complimentary.

"It's all about who you know in this industry," he added, tapping the side of his nose. "Connections and contacts are as important as knowledge and talent."

Maybe he was right, but it didn't make me happy to think that connections and contacts were the way to achieve success. I mean, I had both of those through Dad, but I wanted to make a name for myself because of my talent not just because of who I knew.

My phone started vibrating in my bag. I dug it out and saw Mom's photo flashing up.

"See you guys later. I've got to take this."

I accepted the call and then made my way outside to talk in private.

"What a great opportunity, Simi!" exclaimed Mom, obviously very excited at receiving news of the audition from Mr. Pereira. "Your Vice Principal explained the script to me and it sounds great. Imagine us working together – wouldn't it be so much fun? They've asked me to make a short showreel which I'll be sending over to them today."

I could see students filing back into the building – lunch time was over.

"Yes, Mom, sounds great. I'll call you later. Love you."

"*Mmmmmuaw!*" Mom replied, air-kissing me down the phone.

She really did seem uplifted by the prospect of this job. It made me determined to get this role for Mom.

I would do the right thing.

*

I only had to wait two days to get confirmation of the audition being held mid-December, just before the Christmas vacation. I was going to try my best. Landing the part would mean Mom would be in a happier mood during the winter break.

TAKE ELEVEN

On the day of the audition, I waited in the Academy reception for a BA driver to take me to the Mumbai film studio to meet Mom. I'd expected to be given lines to learn but there was nothing. I wondered if Hollywood auditions were a bit more structured than Bollywood ones. Ours tended to be quite unpredictable.

After a 90-minute journey, I was so glad to see Mom when I got to Daya Film Studios. She was waiting for me outside the entrance. She looked so pretty in a pink anarkali dress that sat just above her ankles. Her yellow dupatta with gold trim complemented the dress so nicely. I went and gave her a tight squeeze.

"Oh, you missed me that much, huh?"

I nodded and clung to her a bit longer.

"Let's go inside," she said.

I followed her to the room where four groups of moms and daughters were already waiting. The girls were all different heights – one looked really tall while one looked tiny. I couldn't guess their ages but anything between nine and thirteen seemed about right.

My mom was the prettiest of the moms, I thought to myself. When it came to high glam, I rarely found anybody who could outshine her.

A man dressed in jeans, a white T-shirt and brown leather chappals breezed into the room a few moments

later and introduced himself.

"I'm Taran, the casting director," he told us. "For this movie, we're looking for real moms and daughters because it's a great marketing angle. It adds a lot of intrigue."

I could see Mom glancing at her competition in the room with a side-eye.

"Now," he continued. "The mother-daughter duo is central to the project. The girl's name is Pinky...and, well, she will only wear pink."

I looked at Mom who knew what I was thinking. She gave me a gentle elbow nudge, urging me to keep listening.

Taran went on: "The movie is a thriller. It will probably be rated PG-13, so most of you won't be able to watch it when it's released. And there will be no songs in it either. It's not your usual Bollywood film, for sure."

I frowned – what was the point of being in a movie you couldn't watch? And one with no songs! That was ridiculous.

The other girls didn't look thrilled either. One of them was wearing a pink party dress, a pink headband and white Mary Jane shoes with a pink strap. I could see her in the role already.

"I'm not sure I want to be in a scary movie, Mom," I

whispered. “I hate horror films.”

“Shhh,” Mom said. “It’s not scary – it’s a thriller. And it’s just a job. Actors do whatever the job demands.”

“But no songs? That is—”

“Enough, Simi,” she scolded. “Stop moaning.”

Taran popped outside and came back wheeling in a rack of – imagine my horror – entirely pink outfits. It was like a Barbie rack. There was a neon jumpsuit, a frilly party dress – similar to the one the girl opposite me wore – and some Indian styles like lehengas and Punjabi suits.

“We don’t usually bring costumes to auditions but the pink theme is so central to this movie, we thought we’d use them to enhance the mood of the auditions. Girls, take an item that’s closest to your size, then head to the changing rooms. The audition will begin once you’re dressed.”

“What about us?” one of the moms asked. “Will we also have nice clothes for the audition?”

“No, madam, you will not,” Taran swiftly corrected her. “Only the girl has to be seen in pink as it is central to her character. That’s it.”

She mumbled something under her breath and then settled back in her chair, helping herself to a handful of crisps from her plastic carrier bag.

All the excitement I'd felt when I'd arrived and seen Mom had evaporated into thin air. I wasn't comfortable with any of this.

Mom nudged me forward toward the rack while I resisted by keeping my feet planted firmly on the floor. The girl in pink – whom I'd privately nicknamed Real Pinky – rushed forward to select her dress first.

"Why does she need an outfit when she's already wearing pink?" I whispered to Mom.

Mom smirked and shrugged her shoulders. "You next," she said, her hand again on my back, gently forcing me to move.

I didn't budge. I let the other two girls help themselves first and then opted for the neon jumpsuit. I usually loved all-in-ones but this piece was pretty hideous with its 80s-style shoulder pads. The alternatives looked way worse.

As we filed out of the room to the changing rooms, three casting directors walked in and took up their seats at the long table. At this point, the nerves really began to kick in.

I wasn't feeling this role, this outfit, this character. It was the opposite of everything I liked about movies in general and Bollywood in particular. I didn't care for thrillers or horror films. I didn't care for movies with no songs. And I definitely didn't care for a character who only wears pink.

I emerged from the changing rooms wishing I were invisible or at least hoping this ordeal would be over soon. I couldn't even glance at myself in the mirror. I looked ridiculous.

This was so embarrassing. All my friends would laugh so hard if they saw me right now. The thought was making me want to run from the scene.

But I had to stay strong for Mom. Who knew when her next opportunity would present itself? I also liked the way she was bubbly and happy now. I didn't want her to go into one of her depressed moods where she would lie down and hibernate for days on end.

A wardrobe assistant led us back into the room where our moms had been moved to one side. In the center of the room was a small chaise longue.

Taran took over the room once again. "Wonderful to see our auditionees looking the part already!" he beamed.

Real Pinky looked excited. The other two girls gave little away and I guessed I was looking distressed or horrified because Mom kept pointing to the sides of her mouth, reminding me to smile.

"I need to explain what we want you to do. Your moms

will come and lie on the couch and you just need to say 'Yes, Mommy' in a kind of zombie-like way and then turn to stare at your mom. You need to look like you've been hypnotized. Your mom will then ask you another question and you'll say 'Yes, Mommy' again. See, easiest audition ever," he chuckled.

I think I'd already fallen into a hypnotic trance. I couldn't understand what this was and how I'd become a part of something so weird. It definitely sounded like a horror film to me. I shuddered. I turned to look at my mom, as though she might pick up on the vibes and rescue me, but she looked fully invested.

Real Pinky and her mom were up first. The casting directors had their score sheets in front of them. Whatever it was that they wanted us to do, I sensed that this mother and daughter duo was doing it perfectly. She said "Yes, Mommy" in a really creepy way, then turned her head very slowly to stare at her mom.

Thankfully, the auditions didn't last long. Each one was over within five minutes. As the third girl got up with her mom to take her turn, I began to feel a little queasy.

I wanted to do this for Mom but I didn't want it for myself. It was the worst thing I could think of. I didn't want to be in a movie I was embarrassed or ashamed of.

I had a few minutes to decide. I looked at Mom, the judges and then around the room at this bizarre setup.

I made up my mind.

We were called up.

Mom sat on the sofa and did a really convincing take of someone feeling under the weather. She rolled her eyes and dabbed her forehead, as though she had a fever and was sweating. I stood obediently on one side. Mom spoke: "Pinky darling, can you get me some pills for my headache?"

This was where I was supposed to say "Yes, Mommy," and then turn my head very slowly, chillingly, to look at her.

"Yes, Ma," I said meekly, deliberately using the wrong words and deliberately keeping my volume low.

Mom's eyes flashed a little as she looked at me.

I turned to face the front again. "Pinky beta, can you get me some water?" I was impressed with how she was making her voice sound croaky.

"Yeah, Mom," I said in a small voice.

Taran looked over at his assistants and furrowed his brow. He made some notes.

"Thank you all for your time," said Taran loudly when it was over. "We'll let you know if you've made it to the next round very soon. Please return your costumes to the

wardrobe assistant. Have a safe journey back."

I rushed into the changing rooms so I could get in and out fast. I wanted to escape this place. I knew Mom must be so disappointed with my effort and I wasn't sure how I would explain it to her.

I found it even more unnerving when she didn't say a word after we'd left Daya Film Studios. She put on her big black sunglasses and looked out of the window the whole journey back to the ferry.

I wished I had the courage to tell her my thoughts and feelings about the role.

I'd been full of confidence and self-belief in Grade 6. It was so straightforward – I would train to become an actor and I would one day become one. But this year, everything seemed to be going wrong. I wasn't sure I liked acting; I was less certain I was even vaguely good at it. I was suffering B-Tunes withdrawal symptoms and felt like I had no passion or sense of direction.

How long could I force myself to do things I didn't enjoy just to please my parents?

It was just before I was about to say goodbye to Mom and board the ferry back to Kohinoor Island that she spoke.

"That was a weak effort," she said in a way that left no doubt about her bitter disappointment.

"Huh?" I gulped. "Umm, I tried my best." I was shaking as I spoke. My mouth felt dry.

"Really?" she asked. "They couldn't hear you speak and you used the wrong words even though you only had two words to say. You completely messed up the easiest audition you'll ever get in your life."

Ouch. That felt like a punch. It hurt. But it was true.

Even if she hadn't said it, the disappointment was etched all over her face. Of course she was mad at me. And why wouldn't she be? I'd let her down, wasted her time too. She'd come all the way from Hyderabad with these happy dreams and I'd shattered them.

I kept my head down and although she allowed me to give her a hug as I got ready to board the ferry, she turned her face the other way.

TAKE TWELVE

I couldn't stop thinking about Mom over the next couple of days. I felt so sad that I'd let her down. Did I do the right thing? I wasn't so sure anymore.

I hadn't even told Joya the whole truth when I'd reached my dorm on the night of the audition. I'm sure she would have been horrified to hear that I'd purposely messed up an opportunity my mom was depending on. I mean, who would do that?

I was feeling really conflicted about acting. For as long as I could remember, acting had been presented as the perfect path for me. For the first time in my life, I wondered – *truly* wondered – if it was the only path, or more importantly, the right one.

After class on Tuesday, I didn't feel like going back to my room. Joya would most likely be at the Noise Zone with the boys anyway. They didn't tell me this, but I overheard her talking to Raktim on the phone.

I decided to go and practice the piano in the Performance Hall. I sat down and began playing. I wasn't in the mood for happy tunes so I played the most impossibly sad song I could think of which made me feel

even worse. The emotions got the better of me and tears welled up in my eyes.

I had to snap out of it.

I took my phone out of my bag and messaged Jai. He always made me feel happy and I knew he wouldn't judge me.

Hey Jai, I began. I could see he was online. *I messed up an audition.*

Hey, he replied, followed by the handwave emoji. *Bummer. How?*

Ugh... I went 2 an audition w Mom for a mom & daughter role but it was a horror film!!!

Horror? he asked, followed by the scream emoji. *Crazy! Then wot?*

I decided it would be quicker to Facetime him instead. "Well, I found out I'd have to wear pink dresses for the whole movie and there were no songs at all. Like, no songs whatsoever! So I deliberately messed it up so I wouldn't get the part... My heart just wasn't in it."

"You meant to fail?" he laughed.

"Yeah, I know. It's so bad of me," I sighed.

"I think you did the right thing."

"You do, Jai?" I stood up and began pacing around the room. "Even though Mom wanted the role so badly? I feel like I've been so selfish."

"Your mom wanted the role but you didn't, and it had to be right for both of you, no?"

I was so relieved to hear this.

"Also it sounds like such a horrible part," he told me. "I can't imagine you doing a role like that. And in pink!"

I was so grateful for my chat with Jai. He made me feel that my decision hadn't been quite as selfish as I thought.

I promised myself I'd put the Pinky nightmare out of my head and focus on the things that mattered. Thankfully, it wasn't long before something came along that put the whole debacle out of my head.

I'd found school trips to be exciting ever since I was a young girl, but this one looked to top them all. A group of us were off to see a real-life music recording session at Blockbuster Studios. Since we were so close to choosing our subject options, all Grade 7 students were being given a real flavor of every aspect of filmmaking from wardrobe to cinematography to dialogue writing to music production. Mr. Joshi was accompanying us and I'd decided not to shy away from asking questions this time.

Thirty of us lined up to board the minibus that would transport us from Kohinoor Island across the Arabian Sea to the mainland. I was really happy when Zeeshan

offered me a seat next to him at the back of the bus. He was wearing his "Dan the Man" baseball cap.

"Nice hat," I smiled.

"Thanks – and I downloaded DJ Dan's new song. Wanna hear?"

I nodded with a smile. It felt a little more like old times already. As we set off, we listened to the song and then spent a while discussing it. It was nice to be sharing music with him again. I'd missed that a lot.

We arrived at Blockbuster Studios at 11am. It was a fair bit hotter on the mainland than on Kohinoor, probably because of the breeze we got on the island. I took off my BA blazer and folded it neatly before putting it away in my rucksack, and Zeeshan removed his cap which I offered to look after for him. We had to keep our ties on though no matter where we went. The BA logo was emblazoned on them in shiny gold thread.

"I want you all to listen to instructions today," said Mr. Joshi as we formed two lines of fifteen students each. "You are representing the Academy and we will not tolerate any bad behavior or disruptions of any kind. Be respectful and appreciative of this opportunity. Is that clear?"

"Yes, sir," we all nodded.

I was eager for the tour to begin. I simply couldn't

wait to see the setup of the studio and discover all the instruments and musicians in there.

After being given refreshments in the reception area by the Blockbuster team, we were led to a room that had been prepared especially for us.

"I'd like you to welcome Mr. Emran Satyajit, the Studio Manager," said Mr. Joshi. Emran looked like he was in his forties but dressed like he was a lot younger. He was wearing a white shirt with track pants – a strange combination but it worked in a way.

"Please call me Emo for short," Emran began as he addressed our group.

"Yes, but out of respect, we should add "ji" to your name, so can we call you Emo ji?" asked Zeeshan.

"Emoji! Emoji!" The students burst out laughing at Zee's joke. Even Mr. Joshi was grinning but trying not to.

"Good one," said Emo, who didn't look offended but didn't seem to find it particularly funny either. "Enough already," he said firmly. "Pick up the notepads and pens in front of you. It's time to begin."

Emo used the smartboard to talk us through the different stages of music production. We learned about song writing, arranging, tracking, editing, mixing and mastering. I found it all fascinating, especially the part where he told us what separates music from the east from western music.

"Indian classical music is distinct from western classical," he explained. "Western classical is written for a group of musicians or an orchestra by a composer. Indian classical is played by a soloist and mostly improvised around a scale called a Raga."

I scribbled it all down. I wondered how and why these two different musical forms had evolved like this. Being self-taught, I found that although I knew how to do things, I didn't always understand why I was doing them that way.

"After this session, you'll all be able to watch a movie song being recorded featuring playback singers Mehreen and Tushar," Emo added.

"Ooh, I love Mehreen!" cried Joya, while other students gasped.

I was excited. They weren't the biggest names in the business but they had good reputations and bright futures ahead of them.

"The movie is produced by Shashi Kumar and is as yet untitled," Emo informed us. "Before we head to the seats in the Viewing Gallery we're going to look back at the careers of the great music composers of Bollywood movies."

Everyone watched the images on the screen switch

from one great personality to another.

I raised my hand half-way thróugh. "Why are they all men?" I asked bluntly.

"There are maybe one or two females in this list I compiled," he responded.

"Simi has a point though, Emran. What's the percentage?" asked Mr. Joshi. I could always count on Mr. Joshi to come to my rescue.

"Ummm," Emo looked uncomfortable. "Maybe 5%?" he offered.

"One in twenty?" remarked Mr. Joshi. "I don't think so. I think one or two in 100. So 2% tops?"

"No way!" squealed Narinder, looking shocked. "Why is it so low?"

"Maybe the men have more talent?" Zeeshan said loudly before bursting into laughter.

I gasped. How could he even think such a thing, let alone say it?

"Zeesh, that's not fair," said Raktim.

"I second that," added Joya, looking offended.

"I'm just kidding!" he laughed. "Can't you tell?"

I decided to ignore Zeeshan. I turned back to Emo and Mr. Joshi. "Seriously then, why are there no women in music production?"

Both Emo and Mr. Joshi looked stumped. Emo looked

at his watch. "Oh, look. It's time to head to the gallery," he said.

As we filed out of the room, I could hear groups of students talking about it.

"It's true though," said one girl. "All the music composers in Indian movies are men."

"Yeah, but like Zeeshan said, maybe women just aren't as good at music," replied a boy.

I glared at Zeeshan. "See! You said it, now they're all saying it!"

"I've already said I was kidding!" He put his hands in the air.

We shuffled along toward the studio. I knew this wasn't the right place to have this debate but I really wanted to get to the bottom of it.

We took our seats in the Viewing Gallery, a beautiful space with clear glass walls on all sides.

"The walls are soundproof," Emo informed us. "You can hear the sounds from the studio through the speakers and you can see what's happening through the glass. But nobody can hear us from there."

I was so excited to see violinists, tabla players, sitar players and an electric guitarist make their way in and get into position. Some of the students clapped excitedly when they caught sight of Mehreen and Tushar. A few took photos and the singers were kind enough to wave and blow kisses through the glass.

Once the song recording got underway, I had goosebumps. To witness the singers harmonizing with the musicians was magical. The music composer, who I didn't recognize, was using his hands – like a conductor – to guide them. It was incredible how everybody just focused on their own part, but simply by performing together, managed to create something so amazing. That was how I used to feel when B-Tunes and I performed. Being in sync, musically, with others was one of the best feelings you could have.

"That was too good!" I said to Raktim who looked awestruck too.

"Can we meet the music composer, Emo ji?" asked Zeeshan.

Everybody suddenly got very excited and the chatter grew loud.

"Okay, okay!" said Mr. Joshi. "Please be quiet and listen to Emran."

"We can't allow all of you into the room – only a handful at a time," Emo decided.

Almost every student's hand shot up in the air, including mine.

"We can choose maybe five pupils to go in and speak

to Parag Shah. A great opportunity if music is what you plan to do with your life."

I couldn't help myself. I put my hand up, waved it around, jumped up a little. I just stopped short of shouting "Me, me, me, me!"

Emo picked out the students – 1, 2, 3, 4...

Zeeshan, Joya, Raktim and I jumped up together.

"The young man over there with curly hair."

"Yes!" Zeeshan punched the air.

I felt deflated as I watched them go through to the other side of the glass door.

"Why do all the boys get to go in?" said Nuzhat suddenly.

In my disappointment at not being chosen, I hadn't noticed this. "Five out of five are boys!" I moaned.

"I'm sure all you girls will get an opportunity too," said Mr. Joshi.

I wasn't sure. I folded my arms tightly.

"And I doubt gender is the reason they got selected," he added.

"Oh," remarked Joya. "Was it because of their natural good looks...? I mean, I love Zeeshan but I don't recall Emo ji choosing on any kind of merit."

I smirked. Joya was right.

The speakers had been switched off so we couldn't

hear what was being said inside the studio. I could see Zeeshan raising his hands really fast on several occasions. Some of the others were doing it too. Was it a quiz? He seemed to be speaking to Parag Shah at length.

"So why are there barely any music composers who are female?" I asked Mr. Joshi as we waited for the group to come back and join us. It was bugging me. After seeing all boys in that room, it was bugging me even more.

"Umm." Mr. Joshi seemed to be at a loss. "I wouldn't like to say it's down to a lack of talent," he replied carefully. He obviously didn't want to be set upon by the girls. "Perhaps a lack of opportunity or a lack of desire?"

"Why would there be a lack of desire?" I questioned. There was certainly no lack of it on my part.

"Some jobs are traditionally 'male' and others traditionally 'female,'" Mr. Joshi offered, using his fingers as quotation marks. "Maybe women don't feel welcome in traditionally male spaces. Or maybe there aren't enough female role models so they don't think it's an option for them."

"A makeup artist is a traditionally female role but there are loads of males doing that now," I countered. "Same for stylists and choreographers."

Mr. Joshi thought about it and nodded.

"But for jobs that men have traditionally done – like

DJing, music production, cinematography, stunts and stuff like that," I went on, "girls barely get a chance."

"I think this debate is for another day, Simi," concluded Mr. Joshi. "It's too complex to have here."

Just then, Emo brought Zeeshan and the four other boys back in. They were excitedly chattering about the equipment they'd seen and the discussion they'd had with Parag Shah. Zeeshan had the biggest grin on his face. I was sure I was going to get all the details later.

"Can some more of us go into the studio now?" I asked Emo.

"No, we're out of time," he replied flatly.

It wasn't fair. And judging by the moans and groans that bounced around the room, the other girls felt the same.

Emo went over to Mr. Joshi to have a quiet word. Mr. Joshi was nodding and smiling, looking really pleased.

"Just before we head off for lunch and then back to the minibus, Emran has just told us that Mr. Parag Shah has kindly offered to give Zeeshan – who won the mini quiz in there – five mentoring sessions. What a kind and generous offer!"

What? I thought to myself. I hadn't even had the chance to enter the quiz! Or share my knowledge and enthusiasm!

I was pretty sure that it was this kind of attitude that had led to there being so few female music composers in Bollywood and I didn't know how on earth someone like me could even begin to challenge it.

TAKE THIRTEEN

The last week before the Christmas break was careers week and the Academy was hosting a big careers fair to help us choose the subjects we wanted to study during Grades 8-10.

I logged on to the BA website and booked appointments with the different teachers. I'd pretty much decided which subjects I would take, but there were a few questions I needed answering.

On the day of the careers fair, my very first – and most important – appointment was with Mr. Joshi.

The hall was really busy with students excitedly walking around, trying to work out who they were meeting first. Joya had rushed off to hand in some homework but had told me she'd meet me in the hall in half an hour. Zeeshan and Raktim hadn't booked slots fast enough so they had to wait until the afternoon for their meetings.

"Hello, Simi," Mr. Joshi smiled as I took the seat facing him. "My super talented student, I hope you'll continue with music – even if you don't want to do it beyond Grade 10."

I smiled back nervously. I knew the time had come when I was going to have to say something. All the ups and downs of the semester had been running through my head – Bela and Marc looking embarrassed at my terrible acting, Miss Patel holding me up as an example of what *not* to do in class, my mom feeling let down by the horrific Pinky audition. But on the flip side, all the joy music had brought me – everyone dancing to my song at Producer Uncle's party, the elation I'd felt when the tune I'd helped write went down so well at the OBAs, and the legendary Mirza Choudhary calling me Melody Queen in front of the paparazzi. I had struggled so much with this decision but I couldn't keep my secret ambition hidden any longer. I knew now was the time. My heart was thumping as I planned to figure out whether my love of music could possibly, just possibly, turn into a career.

"Thank you, sir," I said politely. "I want to carry on with music but I'm not sure my parents want me to."

"Why? You're fantastic at it."

The corners of my mouth turned up. I could definitely do with some praise right now.

"Even if you plan to become an actor and have a career that's nothing to do with music, it's such an integral part of our movies," he told me. "The more musical knowledge you have, the better you'll be at whatever role you play in the industry."

That wasn't quite what I wanted to hear. I grinned nervously. I wanted to elaborate but the words weren't flowing. I opened my mouth to say something but no sound came out.

I wasn't brave enough.

"Thanks," I muttered. I rose from my chair and picked up my notepad and pen.

"You look a little troubled, Simi," he commented. "Is everything okay?"

"Yes, sir."

"There must be questions you want to ask me," he added, encouraging me to speak up. "We have five more minutes – best to use the time?"

He looked at the empty seat. I sat down again.

"Sir, what if I wanted to pursue music as a career?" Finally, the words tumbled out.

Mr. Joshi looked surprised. Pleasantly surprised.

"Well, you have a fantastic musical sense, a great understanding of rhythm, and you play instruments," he replied. "Your voice needs some development though."

"My voice?" I asked, confused.

"Yes, if you want to be a playback singer, you'll need tutoring in classical singing to develop your vocal range."

"But I don't want to be a playback singer, sir. I don't

think I could ever be a great singer."

"Oh?" Mr. Joshi looked intrigued. "Then what do you have in mind, Simi?"

I gulped and then blurted it out. "I want to be a music composer, sir."

He paused. A long, gut-wrenching pause.

I felt hot. I was sure I was sweating.

"A music composer?" He repeated the words again as though he may have misheard.

I felt really small. Was this like saying you want to be president when you're seven years old and everyone just laughs? But I'd said it now. I had to believe in myself.

"I like to compose music. I love Bollywood songs. And I think I'd be good at it."

Mr. Joshi cleared his throat. "It's really hard to become a composer," he said eventually.

"Hard?"

"Well, yes," he went on. "There are only a handful of successful composers at any one time. What I mean to say is, at any given point in time and during any decade, there are fewer than ten composers or duos who get the bulk of the work. The rest struggle to earn a living."

I nodded. "But if they'd all thought like that, would any of them have gone for it at all?"

Mr. Joshi smiled. "My point is that the cards are

stacked against anybody who wants to be a Bollywood music composer. Being female makes it even harder. I want you to take music as an option, but your parents have the right idea if they sent you to the Academy to train to be an actor."

I felt like somebody had squeezed my chest and removed all the air from my lungs. It had taken a lot to admit to Mr. Joshi what I had in mind, and he had always championed me. If there was one person who I had expected to support me, it was my own music teacher.

How stupid was I to even think this was going to work out for me?

"Yeah, you're right, sir," I said, rising from my chair. "Thank you."

I kept my gaze to the floor as I moved off. I felt confused and disappointed. I could feel my cheeks burning.

Even though I was supposed to go and meet my English teacher, I quickly turned on my heel and headed for the exit. I walked purposefully, except I didn't know where I was going. My pace quickened as I saw a door leading to the grounds.

I passed a female cleaner who was putting her equipment away in one of the cleaning cupboards and then a male gardener who was neatly trimming the rose

bushes outside. Did everyone do jobs dictated by their gender?

I walked by with my head bowed, hoping they wouldn't notice the tears in my eyes. They were looking at me a little strangely, probably wondering where I was going. I didn't know myself. All I knew was that I needed to get as far away from the school as possible.

I knew I wouldn't be able to exit the grounds without the alarms going off but I found the farthest point possible. I had to go down lots of small, winding steps. I could almost feel the altitude changing as I descended, getting closer to the sea. I reached the wooden slatted fence that was way too high to climb – but where would I go anyway?

I had to clear my head. I couldn't believe that my own music teacher, who claimed I was one of the most talented students at the Academy, was telling me not to pursue my musical dreams.

I peeked through the gap in the fence and could see the Arabian sea in the distance. The surface glistened as the rays of the sun bounced off it. It was so peaceful and calm – the complete opposite of what I was feeling.

Was anybody on my side? Mom was obviously still upset with me as she hadn't sent the usual texts asking me little things about my homework, exams and auditions. Mr. Joshi had just nipped my dreams in the bud way before they'd had a chance to flower and my bandmates didn't even care that they'd lost a band member. Could they not see I was hurt at being excluded?

I thought back to the Academy's motto: *We hone your talent so you can shine like a star*. Why was my natural talent for music not being honed? Wasn't it Mr. Joshi's job as a teacher to encourage students? Regardless of their gender?

I made a decision.

I would talk to my bandmates and finally tell them how I felt. Once I had them on side, I would talk to Mom and Dad. Hopefully my parents would also come on board and steer me toward my dream career, despite their inevitable disappointment.

That could happen, couldn't it?

I don't know how long I stood down there, lost in thought, but I trudged back up to the main buildings when the sun was starting to feel too hot.

"There you are!" came an anxious voice as I reached the Swiminoor. "We've been looking everywhere for you!" It was Zeeshan.

"She's here!" he shouted to Joya and Raktim who were running toward us.

I stayed silent.

"Simi!" said Joya as she reached me. "What happened? I was worried sick."

"What's wrong, dost?" asked Raktim. "Has something happened?"

I shook my head.

"So?" Zeeshan huffed. He was out of breath from all the running around.

I couldn't speak. The three of them were looking at each other. They seemed concerned.

"Sim, Mrs. Arora was looking for you," Joya said. "You missed your appointments. I told her you'd dropped your phone and had to go back for it."

"We were worried about you," said Zeeshan.

It was nice to hear that he still cared. I'd started to doubt it. Joya linked her arm with mine and the four of us walked back under the glare of the sun toward the cafeteria.

My heart was thumping with a mixture of nerves and excitement.

"I need to talk to you guys," I said as we took our seats.

"Sure, Simi, you can tell us anything," Raktim said.

Zeeshan pulled the ring on his can of lemonade. "What's the news?" he asked, taking a gulp.

"Umm, not news exactly," I replied, biting into my doughnut and licking away the sugar that clung to my lips. "Just about my options," I began gingerly. I paused. "I'm not so sure I want to do acting anymore."

Joya took a sharp intake of breath. "*What?*"

"Are you leaving the Academy?" Raktim asked.

"Oh no!" I replied. "Nothing quite as dramatic as that."

"What do you mean you don't want to do acting? You've always wanted to be an actor. You told me that the first day I met you!" said Raktim.

"Well, what else can you do?" asked Zeeshan. He pushed away the hair that was falling over his forehead.

"Music," I whispered. I don't know why I mumbled it.

"Music?" Zeeshan repeated.

I nodded.

Joya and Raktim didn't say anything.

I didn't want to finish my doughnut anymore. I was feeling uneasy.

"But what in music?" asked Zeeshan. "Your parents are actors and you had it all mapped out. What will you even do in music?"

"The same as you," I said, hoping he'd offer some support.

"The same as me?" questioned Zeeshan. "Compose

music?"

"Yeah, same," I commented.

Zeeshan and Raktim glanced at each other.

"You have the talent but..." Zeeshan stopped.

"But what?" I asked, taking a sip of my banana smoothie.

"But..." he kept stopping as though he couldn't find the right words.

So I found the right words for him. "But...I'm a *girl*?"

Joya frowned. She didn't like it either.

Zeeshan nodded. "It sounds wrong to say it but, yeah. How many music composers are female?"

"Not many," I said, snapping a little. "But that doesn't mean there can't be some in the future!"

There was momentary silence.

"But you can only hope to do what people will let you do," was Zeeshan's offering.

"What does that mean?" asked Joya.

"Well, girls aren't expected to become music composers so the chances of becoming one are really slim, no? Isn't it better to study something you can make a career of?"

I was stunned at Zeeshan's argument. There may have been some sense to it but I was his friend and I had expected him to be on my side no matter what.

"Do you think I have the talent for it or not?" I asked, looking him straight in the eye.

"Of course you do," he replied.

"Well then!" I said.

"It doesn't mean it will happen just because you have the talent," he countered. "Bollywood doesn't work like that. Life doesn't work like that!"

"Because people won't change!" I shouted. "Including people like you!"

I stood up.

"I've had such a bad day," I started, tears welling up in my eyes. "Mr. Joshi said the same thing as you. That I have the talent, but that he doesn't think I should do it because I'm a girl!"

"She's right, Zee," said Joya. "In this day and age, talent should be the only thing that counts. If we don't change it, who will?"

"See! You're supposed to be my best friend and you've been totally wrapped up in yourself," I said to Zeeshan. "You don't even care if I'm part of the band!"

Zeeshan shook his head. "That's not fair! *You're* the one who wanted to act. It's not my fault you didn't want to perform at the OBAs with us. And *you're* the one who quit our WhatsApp group, so stop being so sensitive!"

"Don't make out that I'm the one being dramatic!"

I told him furiously. "Of course I quit the group – why wouldn't I? I was being treated like an outsider! That time you all went out to Kohinoor town to celebrate the success of the OBAs without me, not even telling me. Then all the rehearsals since then in the Noise Zone without me – there's no reason I couldn't have joined in those at least! Nobody even asked me!" I was finding it hard to continue. I didn't want to burst into tears.

"Sorry, Simi—"

I cut Joya off. I needed to get this off my chest.

"It was *my* work on the melody for the *Dil Se* song that brought it all together. Fine that I didn't get any credit for it but then you all just carried on without me, like I was never even part of B-Tunes!"

I pushed back my chair and ran out of the cafeteria. I bolted down the corridor and out into the gardens. I could hear their footsteps as they chased after me.

"Wait!" Joya called out.

I stopped and waited for them to catch me up. I realized I wasn't done.

"Oh my goodness, Simi!" said Zeeshan. "What has gotten into you? It wasn't like that at all. I didn't mean it to be like that. Why are you crying?"

I wiped the tears away. "Because I have to fight against my family, my teachers, the film industry and also my best friends to do what I want to do!"

Raktim came forward. "That's not true, dost. We thought you wanted to quit – especially when you left the Whatsapp group. We thought you'd made it clear."

"And why did I quit?" I looked at all three of them. "Because you were doing all these rehearsals and not inviting me! I helped you get into the OBAs and you guys got all this glory and none of you could even thank me afterwards, let alone include me!"

They all stood, silently listening to me. Raktim nodded, then looked away. Zeeshan fiddled nervously with his hair.

"You go and celebrate in town with Mr. Joshi and nobody even bothers to tell me! Did you all talk about me at your lunch? Is that why Mr. Joshi has zero faith in me making it in music, just like you?"

I felt stupid for saying that. I doubted they had even mentioned my name at the Kohinoor town lunch but I felt so hurt by their actions that I was just lashing out. I heard a group of people whispering as they looked on.

Raktim, Joya and Zeeshan seemed distracted.

I turned around and was horrified to see a group of students standing behind me.

Right beside an open-mouthed Mr. Joshi.

TAKE FOURTEEN

The end-of-year break had come at the perfect time.

I couldn't believe I'd said all those things to my bandmates. I felt angry at B-Tunes for not supporting me and ashamed about my emotional outburst all at the same time. Needless to say, I was blocking out the part where I'd turned around to see Mr. Joshi standing behind me. I'd been so shocked to see him, I'd run off without giving him a chance to react, making it even more embarrassing.

I'd managed to calm down over the vacation, and Christmas had passed by more or less joyfully. I was now even looking forward to my birthday.

I grabbed a notepad and pen and started writing out my birthday wish list.

"Priya's coming to stay," Gauri told me as she walked by to get to the yard.

"*What!*" I exclaimed, dropping my pen.

"Yes, I heard your mom on the phone," she confirmed. "Ask her."

I slammed my notepad on the sofa and ran to Mom's bedroom. "What's this about Perfect Priya?" I asked.

"Simi!" scolded Mom. "That's no way to talk about your cousin. You should treat her like a younger sister. She's such a good girl. Priya studies hard – she's getting top grades in school. And have you seen her dance? Uff. I think she should enter Dance Starz next year. Maybe she can also get a scholarship like Bela and join you at the Academy."

Ugh, please no!

"Get the spare bed in your room ready."

The last thing I needed right now was perfection staring back at me to highlight all my flaws. I sat down and took a moment to ready myself for what was coming.

Perfect Priya was a beautiful kid with long glossy hair, and so delicate and feminine in the way she moved and spoke. Aside from getting top grades at school, she was excellent at making Indian treats like barfi and gulab jamun. I heard she'd also begun stitching Indian clothes – was there anything she couldn't do?

Oh, yes – she couldn't compose music and she sucked at sports. We had nothing in common.

Even though I was feeling lonely, hanging out with Priya was perhaps...well, *worse*.

Mom was off out again. Today, she was cutting the ribbon for a new Indian candy store opening in a neighboring town. I doubt Mom got paid for these things but the newspapers and Instagram paparazzi would be there so some publicity was on the cards. I just hoped they wouldn't edit her out of the photos this time.

She was wearing a fuchsia sequined lehenga skirt, split to the thigh, paired with a long flowy jacket. The outfit was pretty jaw-dropping but it didn't look like daywear to me.

"Don't you think you're a little overdressed for cutting a ribbon, Mom?" I asked as she stepped out.

Mom flashed a stern look at me and continued on her way.

I spotted my swingball set and decided to take a few swipes at it. I'd worked up a good sweat by the time the Bentley crawled back into the driveway again. In the back seat was Perfect Priya. She stepped out of the car with a big smile on her face. She was wearing a dress, as usual, and she'd definitely grown a few inches. In fact, she was as tall as me.

"Hi, you look different," I told her. I wasn't going to say she looked pretty.

"Hi, Simi!" she beamed as Rajiv opened the trunk of the car to get her suitcase out. It looked massive. How long was she staying?

The last time Priya had stayed was over a year ago. I'd spent most of the time holed up in my studio with a

NO ENTRY sign on the door. She always used to follow me around and I found it annoying. Now that we were in high school, with different vacation periods, I'd barely seen her. She looked like she'd grown up quite a lot.

"Simi didi, this is for you," she said, handing me a box.

"What's this for?" I asked. I had to admit, the box of cookies and doughnuts looked delicious.

"You know Indian families," she laughed. "Mom said I couldn't come empty-handed."

"Well, thanks," I conceded. My mouth was watering. "Should we go in and have some?"

Priya nodded eagerly and followed me indoors where we headed straight for the kitchen. Gauri was dishing up some rice and chicken curry when she spotted us with the box of sweet treats. I opened it and then grabbed two plates.

"Uh oh, no you don't!" Gauri scolded.

"Why?" I asked.

"Because I was instructed to give you both lunch."

"Yes, but Mom didn't say whether lunch comes before or *after* dessert," I said sassily.

Priya chuckled mischievously. She pointed to the back yard. We grinned at each other and then scooted outside with the box. This was not at all how I remembered her!

I handed Priya a doughnut and took one for myself. We ran all the way to the trees at the far end of the yard, stuffing the chocolate-coated treats into our mouths. The sight of Gauri running after us made us laugh so hard!

By the time she reached us, our doughnuts were gone and we were lying on the ground. I had a cramp in my side from laughing so much. Gauri grabbed the box and went back inside, shaking her head. Even when she was annoyed, she never shouted at me.

"Do you think she'll still give us lunch?" asked Priya. "I'm still hungry!"

We both giggled some more.

I realized that this was the first time I'd laughed in ages. Maybe it was too soon to say and perhaps I didn't want to admit it yet, but I was kind of glad my perfect cousin had come to stay.

We spent the next day watching old videos of us as kids, an American teen TV show and, amazingly, messing around in my studio. Priya didn't know anything about making music but she seemed to be enjoying what I was creating. I'd never let her in there before and I liked not having to spend all my time alone.

I was pleasantly surprised to find that she was really calm and patient. But she also had plenty of knowledge about a variety of things – social media trends, astrology

and fashion design to name just a few. We had a lot to learn from each other. I didn't even mind that Mom and Dad were – as usual – out most of the time.

We popped down to see Jai on the second day of her stay, and even though Priya didn't join in with the actual cricket practice, she sat with Viraj and they ate ice cream together. It was nice.

Priya was only staying two more days and I was, strangely, hoping they'd pass by very, very slowly since I didn't want her to go yet.

"Shame you won't be here for my birthday, Priya," I said as we had breakfast. "It's the day after you leave. I'm gonna be a teenager. I can finally have my own social media accounts!"

She took a mouthful of dosa. The thin pancake, made from rice and filled with potato, was my absolute favorite and Gauri was an expert at making it.

"There's nothing stopping me from staying," she commented. "I was going to come back on Saturday with Mom and Dad for your birthday party anyway. I could stay the full week?"

"Really?" My eyes lit up, but I saw Gauri looking at me with a smile so I toned it down. Gauri laughed. All these years she'd been hearing me complain about my cousin and avoiding her. Now, here I was, hoping she'd extend her stay.

"I'd love to stay," Priya smiled. "I wasn't sure you'd want me here so long. I thought you might have plans with your friends and stuff."

I felt a little guilty. I'd often been cold and unfriendly toward her and had stopped returning her phone calls a year earlier, so she'd stopped calling.

"Umm, no plans with friends," I said as we finished our breakfast. I remembered my bandmates again and a sadness came over me.

"Let's get ready and go out in the back yard?" I suggested. Priya agreed.

I put on a pair of shorts and a T-shirt while Priya opted for leggings and a long top with cold-shoulder detail. She looked effortlessly elegant, as ever. We sat on the veranda.

"Now that you're staying, can you help me create my social media accounts?" I asked.

"Yeah, sure!" she said, standing up really fast. "That would be so much fun."

"I need a name for my accounts," I began.

"Oh, okay, let me think." She tapped the side of her head, as though a name was going to magically fall out of there.

"Umm, what's the nicest thing anybody has ever

called you?" she asked.

It took me ages to get there but then it came to me.

It was our eureka moment because Priya jumped up and clapped when I said it.

"Yes! That is *so* perfect for you," she smiled. "Melody Queen it is!"

TAKE FIFTEEN

"There!" said Priya as she made my Instagram account live on the morning of my thirteenth birthday. I'd spent so much time on my music app, I didn't know Instagram that well.

"How do you know so much about Insta?" I asked her. We were sitting on a small sofa in the kitchen, sipping hot chocolate with marshmallows served up by Gauri.

"Me and Mom make so many dance reels," she told me. "Have you not seen our family account?"

I shook my head, so Priya quickly showed me. There were countless cute videos of both of them doing the latest dance challenges.

I yawned. It was only 8am but we'd gotten up as early as we could considering we'd stayed up watching movies till late into the night. I had opened my eyes at 6am and been too excited to go back to sleep.

I stared at my iPhone, scrolling through the posts Instagram thought I might like. The account was now live, but what was I going to post?

"I'm no good at this," I sighed. "The girls who take pics and videos of themselves wearing different outfits

or makeup styles or hairstyles and post them – that's not me."

"What type of account do you want it to be?" Priya questioned.

"I just want to share my music with people around the world," I told her.

I made a spontaneous decision. I created a 15-second post with an image I'd taken of a flower in our yard but added my own music to it.

"Use hashtags," advised Priya. She took the phone from me and added: #music #melodyqueen #flower #mellowmusic. "There, that kind of thing," she said. "If anybody looks for those hashtags, your post may come up."

I nodded, then eagerly stared at my screen, waiting to see what happened.

Ten minutes later, nothing had.

"Okay, let's try something more funky," I said.

We selected a disco beat I'd created at the beginning of the summer, chose another random image and posted it with a different set of hashtags. We chatted for half an hour or so and checked back. It had one random "like."

"It's hardly breaking the internet," I laughed.

"That's not how it works," said Priya sensibly. "It can take so many posts and maybe so many months to get going. You need to follow people and you need followers. So, think of who you want to follow."

I searched for "Mirza Choudhary."

"Done!" I exclaimed proudly.

"That's it?" Priya laughed.

"Yep, just one for now. Oh actually, one more." I clicked on DJ Dan's profile and followed him too. "Just two – one new music, one old music."

I thought for a moment. I found Zeeshan's account and followed it as well. "Just to see what B-Tunes are up to," I told her. "Zeeshan won't know who Melody Queen is. Total of three!"

"You're cool and different," Priya smiled. "So your account should be different too."

Her comments made me feel good, especially since I didn't always get told that being different was a good thing. It was refreshing.

I grabbed a blanket that had been folded up and left on one side of the sofa and draped it over both of us. We browsed Mirza Choudhary's recent posts, liking or commenting on them. Priya smiled at me, her metal braces on full show. This girl was growing on me, I thought. I liked that she was family.

"Hugratulations!" said Mom and Dad in unison as they came into the kitchen with gifts for me. I embraced

them both.

"Your main present is next door," they told me.

I looked inquisitively at Priya as we followed Mom and Dad into the hallway. Dad smiled and pointed to the living room.

"No way," I said, trembling. Priya was grinning. Did she know what it was?

Slowly opening the door and peeking through, I saw the most beautiful black piano wrapped with a big red bow.

I put a hand over my mouth and squeaked "Oh!" It had been my dream to own my own piano since I was five years old, and now, finally, I had one!

I looked at Mom. "I didn't think you'd ever get me one."

"Thank your dad," she smiled. "He told me he was getting one and it was final. Sneaking it in after you both went to bed was a challenge though!"

I gave them both a tight hug and ran over to the piano. What a huge effort it must have been. My heart was full. I sat down on the stool and started playing a tune I had in my head.

"Nice rhythm!" said Priya, nodding her head in time to the beat.

"Come up to the studio with me, Priya," I said

excitedly. "I want to record it today."

Priya followed me upstairs where I quickly set up my computer to start my new project. I selected the right settings, then picked out the melody line on the keyboard. I increased the tempo slightly and had another go. I smiled. It was now playing out just as I had imagined downstairs.

I put my headphones on and played my tune, recording as I did so. I then spent some time on the arrangement: I layered different instruments on top, including violin – my favorite stringed instrument. I experimented with some vocal effects – no words, just sounds. A smattering of drum beats and a couple of edits later, I was ready.

I played the complete tune to Priya. She listened and then, slowly but surely, a smile spread across her face.

"I like it!" she exclaimed. "Play it again."

"Really?" I would ordinarily have pinged it straight to Zeeshan but I wasn't sure I could do that now. We hadn't been in contact since our little war of words in the Academy grounds.

Priya listened again.

"Ooh, I love it!" She listened a few more times. "Simi didi, you know what you need?"

"What?" I asked, wondering what she could possibly

tell me with her serious lack of musical knowledge.

"A dance!"

"Huh?"

"Tunes catch on and become big on Insta or TikTok when there's a dance to go with them."

She was right. I thought of all the famous pop songs, including DJ Dan's big hits. The songs had become monster successes on social media once they had accompanying dance moves.

I was terrible at dancing, though. Priya surely knew that. She stood up.

"Play the tune again," she told me.

I hit the play button.

She shuffled her feet twice to the left then twice to the right, combining her steps with classical hand movements. She then lifted her left leg at a right angle and moved it about in a robotic fashion, while moving her arms. She rolled her hands, clicked her fingers, turned around and jumped up.

I was dazzled. "I didn't know you could do body popping! How did you just do that?" I asked, amazed.

"I don't know," she chuckled. "Probably the same way you just composed that tune!"

That made sense. Writing tunes came so easily to me, I didn't understand how other people couldn't do it. So

Perfect Priya could choreograph too? I laughed. I had completely underestimated her.

We went back downstairs to the music room to finalize the moves. It was so much fun. We laughed and laughed when I couldn't get the popping right. I definitely had two left feet and was really stiff.

By lunch time, we'd nailed it.

"Let's make a reel," said Priya eagerly. "That can be our next post!"

"Oh no," I said, shuddering at the thought. "I'm not ready to be on camera. Why don't I film you doing it? Then I'll post it. My tune, your dance?"

Priya clicked her fingers. "Yay! Perfect! First, we need to give the dance a name."

"A name?"

"Yes. Something catchy... Let's say the word 'Bop' combined with..."

"Bollywood?" I suggested.

"Too long," Priya decided. "How about Bolly Bop?"

I nodded. "It has a ring to it."

We got changed and then quickly put on our shoes.

"Should we go to the end of the yard to make the video?" Priya suggested, looking through the window at the vast outside space. "By those big trees, it'll look like anywhere in the world."

“How’s it gonna catch on with my zero followers?” I asked her.

“Everyone starts with zero,” she replied wisely. “It’s what comes after zero that’s important.”

I hoped she was right.

I positioned the phone on a branch of one of the trees at the right angle to avoid the glare from the sun or anything that might identify our back yard.

We soon discovered that making a 30-second video wasn’t that easy. Either I got the timer settings wrong, so Priya had to start again, or she got the moves confused.

Finally, after forty-five minutes, we’d created a decent video. We added a filter so Priya was a little blurred out and unidentifiable. The effect also made it look a little edgy. The moves, though, were crystal clear. We were elated.

“You killed it!” I whooped.

“Shall we show auntie and uncle?” asked Priya excitedly.

“No, definitely not!” I held her arm to stop her from shooting off. “I don’t want Mom thinking the piano’s to blame for this! She doesn’t like me spending too much time on music. I want my account to be anonymous, just for fun. I want to put music on it and follow music on it. But I don’t want people to know it’s me, so shhhh!” I put my finger to my lips and Priya nodded.

We posted the video and then went back inside.

"Simi, we need to talk to you," said Dad, a little seriously.

"About?"

"Let's go to the office."

I looked at Priya. They couldn't have found out about the Bolly Bop video already, could they?

"Nothing to worry about," said Dad as I followed him into his office. Priya, being respectful, said she'd wait for me in the TV room.

Mom walked in, arms folded, also looking serious.

"We just got a call from the Bollywood Academy. A movie producer needs a last-minute new face for the role of a girl about your age and they're happy to discuss it with you today over a call."

"Today?" I asked, horrified. "It's my birthday, Dad!"

Mom looked sternly at me.

"It won't take more than ten minutes," said Dad. "And you know how you messed up the last audition and how upset your mom was?"

I gulped. I so wasn't ready to audition again right now. What if the role was as terrible as the Pinky one? I didn't think I wanted to waste any more time pursuing acting but I wasn't sure there would be an opening or

opportunities in music either. At the very least, I needed a break from auditions and castings. But after letting Mom down so badly last time, I didn't think I could tell my parents any of this.

"Okay," was the best I could do.

"Great," smiled Mom. "They're calling us now and you'll be free after that."

Thankfully, the audition – held over Zoom – didn't take long and it wasn't difficult. The casting director and producer were super nice and I felt relaxed. Maybe it was because I didn't feel desperate to get the job. I was fairly convinced by this point that I wouldn't ever go on to become an actor so the pressure had eased a little. I was doing it for my parents and I wanted to go back to enjoying my birthday. I made sure I was extra enthusiastic, smiled a lot and said all the right things.

We got the call on Saturday evening, just after I had cut my cake at my birthday party. Mom's face said it all. She was so delighted, she announced it live to all the guests, which was such a crazy Mom-like thing to do. Suddenly people were congratulating me from all sides.

"Hugratulations, Simi didi," giggled Priya, arms held out.

My cricket friends who had been kicking a soccer ball about in the back yard all crowded around me and excitedly began asking me questions. Jai gave me a big hug. I felt like I was in a whirlwind. But I didn't really have time to analyze what it meant in the shock of what came next.

Mom cleared her throat. "I'd also like to announce that I have a part in the same movie. Simi and I will be shooting together!"

I was dumbstruck. Why had my parents kept Mom's involvement a secret? Had they been worried about me sabotaging the audition?

I could see how overjoyed Mom was as she walked around hugging all her close friends.

"The shoot's in Lonavala, you know," I could hear her telling them. "So beautiful up there! So cool in the hills!"

It seemed as though a weight had been lifted off her shoulders. Of course she was happy for me, but I think she was hugely relieved for herself. She seemed to stand taller, be more confident, and all the worry that she usually wore on her face seemed to have vanished.

Whatever my personal feelings, I realized I had to put them aside. I was going to be happy if Mom was happy. I could finally say I'd done the right thing. No, it wasn't what I wanted but pursuing my musical dreams just didn't seem to be an option for me, especially when none of my school friends, family or teachers were supportive

of my ambitions. How would I ever go the distance if I couldn't even get off the starting line? Instead, I felt a kind of peace thinking that everything that was happening was meant to happen.

I was getting ready to enjoy the rest of my party and bask in the praise coming my way, but my phone was pinging me like mad from inside the pocket of my palazzos. I pulled it out to put it on silent but the notifications were coming in fast. They were telling me that the "original sound" of my Bolly Bop reel was being "used."

I opened Instagram and was shocked to find that my music – and the dance moves created by Priya – were going viral.

TAKE SIXTEEN

I scrolled through my phone, eyes scanning all the comments, messages and likes that my account was attracting. My brain was trying to process it all. It was hard to make sense of it.

I stopped and quickly put my phone under my pillow when the door handle to my dorm turned. Joya had just arrived, rolling in her luggage. She gave me a hug and asked me about my birthday.

"Sorry I didn't message you on the day," she said. "I was out with family and didn't get home till late."

"No worries," I replied. "I was so busy, I didn't even think about it." Which was partly true.

I unfolded my dry-cleaned school uniform and hung it up, as Joya unzipped her case and did the same. She then piled her hair on her head in a messy bun, plumped up the pillows against her headboard and sat down, legs stretched out.

As I sorted out my schoolbooks, prepping myself for the week ahead, Joya began swiping away on her phone. I was glad when the sounds of Insta reels filled the air. I didn't like uncomfortable silences.

I jumped up suddenly when I heard a fleeting tune. I turned around to see Joya still scrolling. Around thirty seconds later, I heard it again. Then again.

"Oh, it's that tune," I said casually. "Bolly Bop?"

"Yeah," she commented. "It's everywhere."

I waited for a follow-up comment or opinion but I didn't get one. She simply switched her phone off and started reading a book instead.

I grabbed my phone.

Promise me u r not gonna tell anyone Priya! I messaged.

I hadn't told Priya about Bolly Bop beginning to trend on social media at my birthday party because I'd been in shock and had been worried about my parents finding out. But now that the tune and the dance moves were showing on TikTok, Facebook and Instagram reels, it had become too obvious to ignore.

???? I don't get it, she texted back. *Why wud u not want ppl to know it's ur tune?*

I couldn't be bothered with this back-and-forth texting. I rushed out into the hallway to Facetime her and spoke in a whisper so Joya wouldn't overhear.

"Because I've finally got an acting job that Mom is proud of. I messed up a job for her already and I can't do it again – Mom would be so mad at me. If I get distracted by music now, it won't be easy for me to focus."

"Hmm," sighed Priya. She sounded disappointed. Perhaps she wanted some credit for her dance. I couldn't blame her.

"Please, sis," I said.

"Okay," she said quietly. "I'll keep it between you and me. Our secret."

I put the phone down and closed my eyes. A few days ago, if someone had told me my tune would go viral, I would have been over the moon. But now I kind of wished it wasn't happening because it was pulling me toward the one thing I was making a conscious decision to steer away from. I was itching to tell Zeeshan but I didn't feel like I could. Despite sharing the secret with Priya, I felt confused and alone.

*

I was nice and early for my history class the following day. I sat down, took my textbooks out and waited.

My head jerked up when Raktim walked in and started doing the Bolly Bop. He was beatboxing the tune and, before long, some of the other boys had joined in. I held my breath as I watched. I didn't want to show any hint of emotion.

"Ooh, I looooove that tune," said Ada. She stood up

and started doing the moves, but scurried back to her desk as soon as the teacher walked in.

My mind was racing. I was thinking a thousand things at the same time. I desperately wanted to tell Raktim it was my tune, but then again, I didn't. I was really curious to ask him what he thought about it and I got my moment when the class finished. He waited for me and we headed out together, down the corridor featuring 1950s Bollywood movie posters.

"The Bolly Bop dance is funny," I said, walking fast to keep up with him. We hadn't communicated much over Christmas break but I wanted things to feel as close to "normal" as possible.

"Haha, yeah," he said. "I like that tune."

"Where do you think it came from?" I continued, trying to sound casual.

"No idea," he replied, checking the time on his watch. "What's the topic in geography today?"

"Demographics," I told him as we approached the classroom.

"Come sit with me," Raktim smiled.

That was nice, I thought to myself. I wanted to have a conversation about my outburst at the end of the previous semester, but maybe we needed things to get back to how they were pre-OBAs first.

Mr. Pankhurst, who had just joined our school from the UK, began talking about the population of India. He started breaking down the figures by region and state.

"For socio-economic progress to occur in India, literacy is key," he told us. "The overall literacy rate in this country is low at 77%," he added. "Gender inequality is one of the reasons."

I straightened up. This was of interest to me.

"The male literacy rate stands at 84.7% compared to 70.3% among women. And if you break it down by state," he said, pointing to the smartboard, "Kerala tops the list with the highest female literacy rate of 95.2%, while Rajasthan is the worst-performing state with only 57.6% of women able to read and write."

That was shocking to me. My mouth dropped open further when he told us that in comparison, the literacy rates for both males and females in countries like the UK and USA was 99%.

As the only child of my parents, I'd gotten used to hearing people tell my parents they needed a son to carry on the family name. I'd also gotten used to seeing extended family and friends celebrating the birth of a boy more extravagantly than the birth of a girl, sending out Indian treats or holding lavish parties. But I was shocked and stunned at this information about Indian

literacy. It was bad enough that girls were told they couldn't pursue certain careers. The fact that some girls weren't even allowed to read or write, to go to school, in this day and age was just depressing.

"Can you believe that?" Raktim said to me as we filed out of the classroom at the end. "My Dad told me once that Nepal is like that too. So many girls can't go to school."

We discussed it some more and I was glad to see that Raktim was as unsettled by the figures as I was.

There were still ten minutes to go before our final class of the morning so we decided to pop by the cafeteria to grab a drink.

"Did you make a decision about your subjects for next year, Sim?" he asked as we shuffled forward in the line.

I hesitated.

"Drama," I blurted out.

It wasn't what my heart wanted, but my head told me it was very likely my only choice. I also didn't want another gender debate – and one that I'd be the focus of.

Raktim looked surprised. "Oh? But I thought... You were saying..."

"No," I stopped him. "I had started to think I could study music as I enjoy it and am good at it but my family prefers acting. It was a silly idea."

He stared intently at my face. I tried my best to look convincing.

"Plus, it's in my blood," I joked, trying to lighten the mood. "I'm a star kid, remember?"

"Yo!" came a voice. I turned around and was happy to see Ajay.

"How you doing, Sim?" he asked.

"Yeah, good," I smiled.

"What's new?"

"Ummm, apart from going off on an outdoor shoot to Lonavala next week, not much," I joked.

"No way?" remarked Ajay. "That's cool!"

"Wow!" Raktim commented with a little clap. "Awesome! What's the job?"

"The part's not that big, and I'll be the only child on set," I began. "But it's a movie for Apple TV from what I know."

"That's amazing news!" said Ajay. "Let's celebrate."

He pressed a button on his phone and started doing the Bolly Bop right in front of me as my tune rang out across the whole cafeteria.

Deepa and Monica were walking past with their strawberry frappuccinos.

"Start again!" said Monica, putting her drink down. Deepa giggled and all three of them started doing the

moves. Raktim pulled his phone out of his pocket and started filming.

"I'm telling you, this beat is banging!" Monica said, gently trying to pull me up.

"Uh, it's okay," I laughed nervously. I didn't know how to react. I had gone bright red. I wasn't sure if they could tell but I tried to laugh and giggle it off by pretending I was hot and gulping down my drink.

I was saved by the bell.

As I walked across to my next class, I tried to reflect on everything. There was definitely a part of me that was beginning to enjoy this little success. It was my secret and it was fun to know that only Priya and I knew the truth. I was stunned it was still gathering momentum.

But I was determined not to let it sidetrack me. I had to officially choose my study options by the end of the week.

And the film shoot in Lonavala was just around the corner.

TAKE SEVENTEEN

Lonavala surprised me. I mean, I'd heard about its beauty, but it had never really appealed to me as a travel destination. Apart from nature, what was even there? But that's exactly what was so incredible about it. I was used to the scenic beauty of Kohinoor Island but Lonavala with its hilly terrain and lush green landscape that stretched for miles around, up and down, was thrilling to experience.

The hill station was only about an hour's drive from the hustle and bustle of Mumbai, but being 1000m above sea level, it felt so different.

Mom was acting like a real tourist in her fitted tunic top with pajami – a nod to the 1960s I guessed from the movies I'd seen from that era. She completed the look with black cat-eye sunglasses and a red headscarf tied tightly under her chin. Mom was playing the part of a classic film actress brilliantly.

"You look super stylish," I told her, clicking what seemed like the hundredth picture of her as she posed in front of the third viewpoint of the day.

"Okay, okay," shouted a guy called Rishi who I'd been

told was the Unit Manager for the movie. "Enough selfies – we need to make a move and reach the fort on time so we can get started on the scenes for today."

Rishi had told me that my small role was central to the movie. I wouldn't appear in tons of scenes but the ones I would be in were key. I hoped I would enjoy myself if nothing else.

The movie, *Hum Do*, meaning the two of us, was about a woman with a daughter she is raising alone. She meets and marries a man who doesn't feel any affection toward the young girl. In turn, this puts the marriage under strain. The role was doable for me. It wasn't making me sick to my stomach like the Pinky one. I was going to focus. I was going to use my very best efforts and make my mom and dad proud.

All twenty of us piled back into the minibus to travel to the Lohagad Fort which apparently had the best views over Lonavala. I was googling it as we drove toward it, impressed by its long history across two different empires, the Mughals and Marathas. It dated back to the 17th century. I couldn't even grasp the era Mom and Dad had grown up in let alone over 300 years ago!

"Yes, I starred in several Bollywood movies during my time," Mom was telling Ram Chandra, the actor playing her husband and my father in *Hum Do*.

I put my AirPods in when Mom decided to give the whole minibus a lowdown on every single minor movie role she'd ever landed. I chose a playlist on Spotify and sat back to admire the incredible landscape, peering out the window with my heart in my stomach as I realized how high we were and how far the drop would be if we were to slip down the side of the mountain we were climbing. My ears were hurting a little too.

My phone pinged me – a message from Priya. How did we even have phone reception up here? I laughed as I played the video she'd just sent me – an Insta reel of her and her school friends doing the Bolly Bop in her school playground.

I prayed she was keeping our secret safe.

Another message landed. *PS I haven't told anyone!*

Phew! I settled back comfortably in my seat and must have dozed off because the next thing I knew, we'd arrived at the fort. The minibus parked up as close as we could get to the ancient monument but we still had to climb some stairs. I was starving but Rishi told us we had to complete some filming to make the most of the natural daylight first. His team dished out a few samosas in the meantime and set up a small table with tea, coffee and water.

"Hi, I'm Miriam," said a smiley lady who looked like

she was in her twenties. I liked her dress sense – a long flowing kaftan and matching hijab. "I'm the wardrobe manager for the movie and this is your outfit for the day."

Miriam handed me a pair of jeans with a glittery stripe up the leg, a T-shirt with a picture of a unicorn, and a pair of white sneakers with silver stars on one side.

"How old am I supposed to be in this movie?" I whispered to Mom as we headed for the makeshift dressing area. I knew the answer but the outfit looked as though it was designed for a 7-year-old.

An assistant led us to an area designated as a changing room because a trailer couldn't fit through the narrow, winding entrances.

"You're thirteen," said Mom, checking out her outfit. "Hmm, my costume's not too bad. I don't like the coat very much – it's too matronly."

I laughed. She really was reliving her youth. "At least you have nice black shoes, Mom. Look at my sneakers! I wouldn't have even worn these as a kid."

"Shhh," Mom said as the assistant smiled at us. "It's a job. I don't want your personal likes and dislikes ruining this for us *again*, understand?"

I gulped. I understood only too well. And maybe she had a point. I had to learn to detach myself from the parts I was playing. I reminded myself that I was not going to ruin this for her.

There was more waiting and sitting on uncomfortable chairs until the cameramen, lighting technicians and director had all the equipment set up and positioned correctly.

I was perplexed by all the waiting around on film sets, plus all the makeup day in, day out...and then the weather. I wasn't great with extreme temperatures and I'd seen all those Bollywood actors wearing sarees with sleeveless blouses in the snow or running on the sand in Dubai in the middle of the summer. Crazy!

"Let's get some behind-the-scenes footage while we're waiting," said Miriam. She took photos of a few of us with a selfie stick and told us she'd get them posted on the movie's official social media accounts later.

"Right, let's do an Insta reel."

"Ooh yes, I'd like to try that," said Mom. "Simi isn't the kind of girl who will make those videos with me."

"Oh, yeah?" I smiled mischievously. "Can you play that Bolly Bop tune?" I asked Miriam.

"I sure can!" she replied, digging it up in a flash. "I love the dance moves to this!"

Mom complained she didn't know the song so Miriam expertly showed us how to do the dance. Mom wasn't

bad at it to be honest. I wondered if she'd be happy or shocked to know the truth. I was aching to tell her but terrified at the same time, so I decided against it. I couldn't risk upsetting her.

"I don't want you posting it though, Miriam," Mom told her. "Not until I get the moves perfectly right. We can try again later?"

Miriam nodded as Mom was whisked off to makeup to prepare for a scene.

"Mom, daughter and stepdad are on a day trip visiting Lohagad Fort," the director reminded Mom as she sat in a chair having powder dabbed on her face and her hair pulled back into a low bun. "During the visit, stepdad tells mom that he wants them to consider having a baby of their own."

Mom nodded. "Yes, I've read it and remember that. Go on."

"You need to be really offended at his suggestion. The dialogue that begins, 'But I already have a daughter...' has to convey real shock and emotion."

"Sure," she said. "Understood."

"The climax of the scene is the part where he then tells you that he doesn't consider your daughter to be his daughter...so the couple have a huge fight, in front of the girl."

"Got it," said Mom as she stood up and made her way to the set.

I was enjoying seeing Mom act the complete professional. She was very serious about her work. Totally focused. She excelled at the screaming and shouting part. Mom really looked as though she was mad at her onscreen husband.

All I had to do was look on, tearfully, as I witnessed the argument. It took a couple of takes for me to get it right. Crying scenes were hard. Adding drops of glycerin to my eyes on the final take to make them water helped it look more realistic.

Mom looked happy with all the praise we received when it was time to pack up. I felt an odd sense of satisfaction too. Doing something so professional was making me feel quite grown-up and special. Would this trip mark the moment I fell in love with acting? I was curious to see.

On the way to the hotel, I checked my phone.

"*What?!*"

I rubbed my eyes, stunned to see that I'd gained 4,500 followers on Instagram!

I then googled to see if there were any news items associated with it, and clicked a link at the top of my search list with the headline:

'Bolly Bop is not my tune,' says Mirza Choudhary

Huh? I thought to myself, hands trembling a little. What has Mirza uncle got to do with this?

When I scrolled down to read more, it became clear. "Somebody sent me the video. I really liked the simple and catchy tune so I posted it," said Mirza. "Maybe that helped it go viral. But I can't take credit for it. I don't think anybody knows whose tune it is."

As soon as we'd eaten in the restaurant at the Lonavala Luxury Retreat and Spa, I ran back to my room to look into the analytics of my post. I cleared away the rose petals that were scattered on my bed and carefully moved aside the towel that had been molded into the shape of a swan. I dove onto my pillow and went back to my Instagram post. There were 78,000 views and 771 comments. Most of them were saying how much they loved the tune or people were tagging their friends to alert them to the trend.

"What are you looking at?" Mom asked as she carefully removed her heavy foundation and eye makeup with wipes.

"Just looking up the history of this place," I lied.

"Hmm," she mumbled, "that makes a pleasant change from sports or music."

"Why is Lonavala called a hill station?" A great question to sidetrack Mom, I thought.

"Ah, a hill station is just a high-altitude town," she told me. "It all goes back to the days of the British Raj. When the British ruled India, they used to come to the hilly areas to escape the heat."

"Oh," I uttered. "Like a getaway?"

"Yes," she said, now applying some lotion to her face with small upward motions of her fingers. I watched her for a few seconds.

"Can I say something, Mom?"

She nodded, looking straight at my reflection in the tall mirror.

"You don't need to do all this stuff, you know. You're fine as you are." I put my phone down momentarily. I felt like somebody needed to tell her, and I rarely got an opportunity to be alone with Mom in a chilled-out environment.

"What do you mean?" she asked, turning around to face me briefly before turning back again.

"All this stuff you do... I mean, exercise and everything is good, and I'm proud that you're the kind of mom who wants to stay flexible and healthy..." I paused to think. I needed to choose the right words. "But you don't need to do all this other stuff..."

"What other stuff?" Mom asked.

"Well, I know I'm also gonna get older, but I hope I enjoy every decade. Be the best I can be for the age I am. There's no point in trying to be younger than you are... and you look amazing for your age."

There. I had said it. I waited for the reaction but Mom didn't say a word. She quietly kept on with her routine for a few more moments and then put her toiletries back in the bathroom.

I was partly trying to figure out if I had upset her and partly trying to keep track of all the attention Bolly Bop was getting. I wondered whether I should tell Mirza Choudhary the next time I saw him that it was my tune. Whoever sent it to him, whatever the sequence of events, I concluded that Priya and I somehow owed our secret success to him. Had he not posted the reel, my tune wouldn't have caught on.

I sent Priya a WhatsApp message with a link to the news story where Mirza admitted it was sent to him and he had posted it. I also told her to keep an eye out for any further news items. It was hard for me to use my phone while on set.

"Go to bed," Mom ordered as she got under the covers. She eyed my phone.

I quickly put it away, worried she would get curious

enough to make me show her my messages. I didn't want to imagine that scenario.

I got up to give Mom a goodnight hug and kiss and got back in bed again.

As I was dozing off, I heard a quiet voice.

"You're right," she said simply.

"Huh?"

"About the ageing."

I could hear her, but with the lights out and the darkness in the room created by all that wilderness outside, I couldn't see her.

"Maybe I shouldn't fight it," she conceded. "It's going to be a journey, but I'll try to embrace it."

*

"What a ridiculous time to wake up," I moaned. "It's literally the middle of the night!"

The repeated loud knocks on our bedroom door told me I had no choice. It was 4am and we had to be on set by 6:30am.

Mom didn't look great. She appeared tired and nothing like the glamorous diva who would emerge from this very room thirty minutes later. How she did it so fast surprised me.

"Oh, Radhika, you look nice," said Miriam when we reached the breakfast buffet. Mom had her shades on, no doubt to hide her early-morning eye puffiness, but they just made her look like a star.

While waiting in the buffet line, I snuck a glimpse at my notifications. One stood out. It was a message Priya had sent the night before, urging me to read a news story. I quickly clicked on the link, careful to keep my phone out of Mom's line of sight.

Producers race to be the first to include
Bolly Bop in their movies

My heart was pounding and my face flushed red with panic as I read that musicians were already making covers of the Bolly Bop to use for their soundtracks, all eager to get their versions out first.

I scrolled down the article to a quote by Mirza Choudhary: "As a composer who's had work copied in the past, I feel the person who originally created the song should get the credit. I posted the tune to my account but I don't know who the creator is – I just know that the Instagram account is 'Melody Queen.' Who or what that is, and even if it's the origin of the original, I don't know."

I got through breakfast by taking deep breaths to keep calm. I was bombarding Priya with so many messages but, since it was only 5am, she wasn't replying.

I wondered if I should message Mirza Choudhary from the Melody Queen account. But what if he asked who I was? What if he remembered calling me Melody Queen? He obviously hadn't put two and two together yet. What if he told Mom and Dad? I knew I'd be so upset if Bolly Bop was used in a movie and I didn't get recognition for it.

I wanted to talk to Zeeshan, to seek his advice about all of this, but our friendship wasn't free and easy like it used to be. I could chat to Jai, I thought, but that wasn't going to help me much. And what if he accidentally blurted it out to his parents and they told my dad? No, that was way too risky.

All these thoughts hijacked my mind as we set off for another day's filming. I desperately wanted to stay back in the hotel – a frantic, busy day on a film set was the last thing I needed. But I had no choice.

"Keep up, Simi," said Mom as we rushed to get to the minibus. "Put your phone away – it's unprofessional."

I did as I was told. I was beginning to feel more and more sick every time I looked at my screen.

On Instagram, views of my video, as well as Mirza

Choudhary's post, were going through the roof. Each time I snuck a peek at my phone, I became more aware that Bolly Bop was a full-on trend. Different groups of people from around the world were taking part – families, dance experts, music lovers... Anybody and everybody.

On Twitter, #WhoIsMelodyQueen had begun trending. There were some low-level discussions around whether Melody Queen was a person or a band. Some people were arguing that it couldn't be a female musician and that the account name was designed to mislead people. I didn't even have a Twitter account but the chatter was everywhere.

I had such mixed feelings about it all. I loved that everyone was enjoying my tune and I knew that I should be busy making new ones to cement my place in the music world. Instead, I was stressing about my parents finding out.

I wasn't the only one feeling anxious.

"Why do we have to keep it secret?" asked Priya on the phone. It was our final morning in Lonavala. Mom was having breakfast with the crew on the veranda that overlooked the lake. She'd made friends with a few of them and they were now busily exchanging contact details.

"Because we'll both get in trouble, Priya," I said. "Your parents won't be happy about you dancing on a reel without their permission!"

"That's true," Priya said softly.

"Plus, Mom is so happy on set at the moment, I don't want to make her feel upset or anxious. Our movie shoot is going so well. I think we should at least wait until the shooting is over."

I felt like crying. I didn't know what the right thing to do was and I felt bad that I had involved my little cousin in all the madness.

"Just ignore the whole thing then," said Priya. "Pretend it has nothing to do with you. Nobody has asked me anything about Bolly Bop – they haven't figured out it's me. Some kids at school have made Bolly Bop videos but then they move on to the next big thing. It's not that big of a deal."

"But it is a big deal to me," I countered, moving around to the other side of the veranda where I was out of earshot of Mom. "What if somebody uses it in a movie? Then nobody will ever know the tune was mine. All because I couldn't come forward and own it!"

I blinked hard but couldn't stop the tears from escaping. I wiped them away with the sleeve of my top.

"Simi! Come and have breakfast," ordered Mom.

"Gotta go, Priya. I'll call you when I'm back at the Academy."

I felt a tinge of sadness as we all piled back into the minibus. It was like when you go on vacation with family or friends and then have to say goodbye at the end. I wished I'd been a little more present and not so distracted by my phone and the whole Bolly Bop saga. The *Hum Do* team had been so nice.

Mom would be shooting every day for the next few weeks but I was only needed for a few more scenes at the end of February. I felt sad when I hugged her to board my ferry back to Kohinoor Island. I'd enjoyed spending time with her, practicing lines with her and sharing a room with her. I had seen more of her in these four days than I ever would at home. These had been rare, special moments.

A junior staff member had been sent to pick me up and we sat quietly together for the journey. I avoided using my phone on the ferry – I wanted to disconnect from the crazy digital world.

The chain of events around Bolly Bop – how it had happened, keeping up with what was happening now, and trying to predict what was going to happen next – had left me exhausted.

TAKE EIGHTEEN

I couldn't wait to flop on my bed when I got back to my dorm. As I made my way up, I bumped into Ajay who was with other boys from the cricket team. They told me to come for Saturday practice and I promised I would.

"See you in the Observatory later," Ajay said. "You're coming, yeah?"

"To what?" I asked. But it was too late – Ajay had gotten distracted and had walked off before he heard me.

Just as I entered the corridor that led to my dorm, I came face to face with Raktim, Zeeshan and Joya. I pushed my hair out of my face, conscious I looked a mess.

"Hey, Sim!" greeted Zeeshan warmly.

"Hi," I responded.

Raktim and Joya were carrying musical instruments.

"You guys coming from the Noise Zone?"

"Yeah, we just recorded a song for a movie. An *actual* movie!" said Zeeshan happily. "It was sick! You would've loved it, Sim. It was part of the mentoring program!"

"It was amazing!" confirmed Joya. "Wish you'd been there to watch, Simi."

“Me too,” I said, doing my best to muster a smile.

“Tell us about you then,” Raktim chipped in. “How was the film shoot? Lonavala is the best, right?”

“Yeah it was really good but so tiring,” I replied. It was nice that he’d asked me about it, but I didn’t really want to share more so I just stood there, a little awkwardly.

“Come with us. We’re going to the screening of the OBAs.”

“Huh?” I replied.

“You didn’t know? Oh yeah, you’re not on our WhatsApp—” Joya stopped mid-sentence.

I felt the heat rising up my body. I was a little embarrassed about that.

“Mrs. Arora announced it a couple of days back,” said Zeeshan. “They have the full show now and instead of the regular movie night, they’re screening that.”

So that’s what Ajay was talking about. I agreed to go, but not without feeling a ton of conflicting thoughts and emotions. Did I really want to put myself through that show again? It had been fun, but it had also been pretty difficult to watch my band singing the tune I’d helped them write without any acknowledgement. I was now going to sit through it again... Gah!

Zeeshan leaned in closer and whispered to me. “And I have a little announcement to make about a tune that’s recently gone stratospheric... You're gonna love it."

The color drained from my face. Was he talking about Bolly Bop? He couldn't be! What did he know about my song? But what other tune had recently gone viral? I couldn't think of any. Maybe there had been others that I hadn't noticed due to my obsession with Bolly Bop?

I felt a chill rise up in me. *What if Zeeshan was going to take credit for Bolly Bop and claim it as his tune?* He'd been so self-obsessed recently, and he was so desperate to make it in the music business... The thought was too awful to contemplate. I immediately felt guilty.

We filed into the Observatory and I was surprised at how busy it was. Students from all the grades were taking their seats and excitedly talking about the show.

"Maybe we can go to the OBAs next year?" said one of the Grade 6 girls to a friend. "I saw it on TV – it was awesome!"

"There's that girl who did the soccer tricks," whispered her friend as she pointed at me.

"Recognition at last," Zeeshan joked. I smirked.

I scoured the room looking for Ajay. I hoped I could sit with him to watch our performance together. I caught sight of him just as he was walking in. He waved at me to come over, pointing to some empty seats.

"I'm gonna sit with Ajay," I told the trio. "Watch our

performance together."

"Sure," smiled Raktim.

"Come back and sit with us when it's time for B-Tunes' performance though," said Zeeshan. "I want you to watch it with us, Sim."

"Oh," I replied, taken aback. "Yeah, I will," I agreed, before rushing off to take my seat next to Ajay. Why was Zeeshan so eager for me to sit with them? I needed to talk things through with him rather than always be second-guessing what was on his mind. It was so unsettling.

The lights dimmed and we focused on the huge screen as the show began. There was so much chatter, cheering, and clapping for the segment featuring the Bollywood Academy students.

I really enjoyed watching my routine with Ajay. I was proud of how coordinated we had been on stage. Ajay and I high-fived when it ended. We stood up at Mr. Pereira's request. My bandmates were whistling for me, so I turned to give them a wave.

"A very big well done to Simi who has also landed a major acting role in a movie being made for Apple TV," said Miss Takkar. "No doubt she's on the path to an amazing career as an actor," she went on. "We look forward to seeing the movie when it's released."

Before sitting back down, I looked for empty seats where B-Tunes were sitting but realized they'd all been taken. I was sure Zeeshan would understand. I would cheer really hard for the trio, putting aside any ill-feeling and jealousy, since they had celebrated so joyously for me.

Just before the recording of B-Tunes performing *Dil Se* was to air, the screen paused.

Miss Takkar took to the mic again. "Please allow Zeeshan, one of the founding members of the band, to say a few words. He's been selected for a music mentoring scheme by Bollywood composer Parag Shah and the band has now contributed to a song for a movie!"

Miss Takkar led the applause as Zeeshan stood up. I whistled really loudly.

"I want to thank the school for giving me the chance to pursue this mentoring opportunity – it's been awesome," Zeeshan began. I could tell from his massive grin that he was genuinely over the moon. "To record a song with actual musicians from the industry is so cool. You only get those kinds of chances with this Academy."

Miss Takkar and Mr. Pereira looked delighted. Their eyes briefly locked before Miss Takkar quickly averted her gaze.

He went on: "I want to let everybody know that a lot

of credit for our performance and song at the OBAs goes to Simi. She co-wrote the melody. The ending was hers."

He pointed straight at me and then raised his hands above his head to clap. All heads turned to look at me.

I gasped.

The air I was breathing suddenly seemed to get stuck in my chest. It was a complete surprise. For a second I thought I would burst into tears. I felt totally overwhelmed.

"You did that too?" asked Ajay. "Wow, multi-talented!"

I noticed Mr. Joshi on the other side of the Observatory standing up to applaud. He was the only teacher standing. He looked at me and grinned. I smiled back.

The replay started and I watched with pride at how the band had performed. Joya was fantastic – she got lots of support as she started singing. But Zeeshan was the one all the girls were screaming for. I was sure he could become a centerfold pop star if he didn't want to become a music composer.

The three of them stood to receive the loudest cheers of the evening. I was clapping as hard as I could. Ajay told me that I should be standing up too, but I shook my head. "Enough praise for one day!" I told him.

It took a while for everyone to quiet down, but when

they did, Miss Takkar invited B-Tunes to the podium to speak briefly.

"I'm not sure I should say this here but perhaps there's no better time," Zeeshan began. "Everyone's heard of Bolly Bop, right?"

My heart skipped a beat. The hairs on the back of my neck stood on end at the thought of what was coming next.

Some of the students started beatboxing the tune and a group of girls at the back stood up and started doing the dance.

"Take your seats please and listen to the speaker!" ordered Mr. Pereira.

After some moaning and groaning, the rowdy students quieted down.

"I might be wrong," continued Zeeshan, "but I think somebody at our school wrote that tune."

I froze.

Everyone gasped. Even Miss Takkar went "Ooh!" at the thought.

"No way!" I could hear someone saying.

"But I don't recognize that girl in the video!"

"She looks like a Grade 7 girl I know."

The theories were flying around thick and fast.

"I wonder who it was," Ajay said to me. I shrugged my

shoulders but no words came out of my mouth.

The chatter around me got frenzied as more and more people tried to guess who at the school could have successfully created a viral trend.

Zeeshan went on: "Parag Shah told me that music producers are eager to use it in their movies. If that happens, it's only fair that whoever's behind it should get the credit."

I was so confused right now. One moment I was wondering if Zeeshan was going to falsely take the kudos for my work; the next, I was wondering if he had somehow worked out it was me. But if so, *how*?

"Stand up and be proud of your amazing talent if you're responsible and you're in this room," Miss Takkar piped up. "Share it with the world openly. It would be wrong not to take credit for what rightfully belongs to you."

"I agree," said Mr. Pereira. "I don't know if Zeeshan is right but I can't understand the reason for keeping a major global success quiet. That's why we're here – to let people know how talented we are and to make an impact on showbusiness. Let's do a one-minute countdown. If nobody stands up after sixty seconds, we'll call it a night."

The students started doing a noisy countdown,

shouting out: "60... 59... 58..."

One boy, a Grade 6 student, stood up, waved and got everybody really excited – until he yelled out "Just kidding" to a wave of groans and moans.

"30... 29... 28..."

I had less than half a minute to make a decision. Zeeshan knew it was me, I was convinced. I don't know how, but he did. And he was pushing me to claim it. My heart was telling me to stand up. My head was telling me "No way, you can't!"

"10... 9... 8..."

My heart won.

I stood up, covering my hands with my face. I wasn't sure if I should be doing this. *Why did I do it?*

It was only when the loud screams and cheers threatened to raise the glass roof of the Observatory that I felt like I had done the right thing.

I moved my hands away from my eyes and turned to look at Zeeshan. He was punching the air with a sense of pride.

I felt so emotional as I saw him beaming back at me.

"I knew it!" shouted my friend. "Simi Prasad is the Melody Queen!"

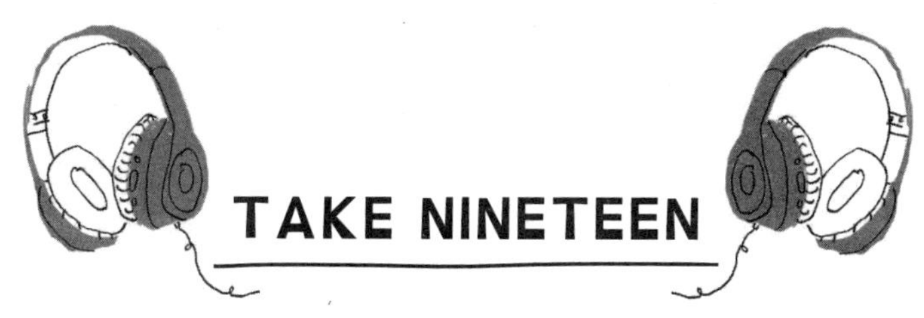

TAKE NINETEEN

"That's her, that's her!"

I rushed along the corridor to get to my class the next morning, and at almost every turn I took, students were either smiling at me, talking about me or asking me for selfies.

The moment after the screening had been amazing. There had been a buzz in the air and it had all been about me and my music! I'd wanted to have a private chat with Zeeshan straight after but there hadn't been enough time and we had soon been ushered back to our dorms.

I was looking forward to the school day being over so I could not only talk to Zeeshan but also have a phone conversation with my mom and dad. I'd already worked out what I would say to them: the viral song happened accidentally and it wasn't going to throw me off my big plans to become an actor, following in their footsteps and making them proud.

In my heart, I knew I loved music way more than acting, but I couldn't bear to disappoint them.

Bolly Bop secret is out @ school! I quickly messaged Priya

as I moved to my next class. *They know it was me! I'm gonna talk 2 Mom & Dad today. Hope they'll be fine & can talk 2 ur parents. I pray uncle n auntie wont b mad.*

I was nervous about talking to my parents but I also felt like a huge weight had been lifted from my shoulders. Keeping the secret had been really hard and I finally felt unburdened and free.

As I pressed "Send," a WhatsApp message pinged me. It was Jai. I opened it and got the best surprise when I saw him doing the Bolly Bop with our cricket team. It was something I would treasure for ever and ever. *How did he know?* I wondered. Social media? Could it move that fast?

U kept that quiet! he scolded in a message. *U owe me an explanation... Better b a good one!*

How did u find out? I questioned.

Thru a news story online about how Melody Queen is a 13 year old girl from the BA. I know u well enough to know it wud be u!

I briefly pondered whether my parents would also already know, but they hadn't called yet so I guessed not.

At school, the news had already spread far and wide. I was the talking point in every class. All my teachers and classmates asked me about Bolly Bop – when I composed it, how I'd managed to keep it a secret for a whole month, and why I did that.

"Everybody was talking about you today, Simi!" Joya exclaimed as she walked into our dorm at the end of the day. "The number of people chatting about the video and then doing the dance was crazy. I can't believe you kept it quiet all this time!"

"I'm sorry about that," I told her. "I just didn't want anybody to know."

"It's okay," she smiled. "I also didn't tell you everything I was up to with B-Tunes. I shouldn't have overlooked your role in the band after the OBAs. I wasn't deliberately being mean. Maybe I was thoughtless and insensitive..." She paused. "We were just so excited about our own success, we got carried away and didn't stop to think about your feelings."

I smiled at Joya. I was so glad we'd cleared the air, but something was still gnawing at me. I needed to find out if the identity of Melody Queen was common knowledge. I got the answer to my question via a quick Google search.

The top result was:

Melody Queen: person behind Bolly Bop viral hit UNCOVERED

The article went on to say, "After much speculation,

the identity of the mystery person behind the viral Bolly Bop tune has been unveiled as a 13-year-old schoolgirl from the Bollywood Academy school on Kohinoor Island."

It must have been the article Jai saw. My heart was beating fast as I scrolled down the page. I breathed a sigh of relief when I saw that there was no picture or mention of my name. Most of the articles I found had some variation of this same story but nothing to identify me. This explained why my parents were still blissfully unaware.

A loud knock on the door got me up on my feet. I ran to open it and saw Zeeshan standing there with a big box of chocolates.

"What are these for?" I gushed, grinning from ear to ear.

"We're celebrating," he smiled.

"Celebrating what?"

"Being friends with somebody famous like you!" he laughed.

"I still can't get over what happened last night," I said, inviting him into our room to sit on the bed. We weren't really allowed boys in our rooms, but a few minutes surely wouldn't hurt. "I mean – how did you know I was Melody Queen?"

"Aha," he said, helping himself to a white chocolate after I'd eagerly ripped open the wrapping. "I just worked it out."

"But how?" I probed. "Melody Queen could have been anyone!"

"Your account was made active on your birthday," he began. "You followed me that day and, as you know, I follow back all my followers. So that gave me a big clue. Then you posted a few tunes. They sounded like your style."

"Oh." I thought back to the day that Priya and I had created the account.

"You also commented on so many of Mirza Choudhary's posts – you wrote "Killed it" and stuff like that. It sounded familiar. Finally..." Zeeshan laughed out loud before continuing, "I noticed lots of comments from the account on Mirza's posts when he released his new song. One comment in particular: 'Hugratulations!'..." Zeeshan was in fits of giggles by now, and Joya had joined in. "Who says that but you? It left no room for doubt."

He had a point. I chuckled when I realized how obvious it must have been to him. So, he'd known all along and I was working overtime to keep it a secret!

"The tune was so cool," he said. "Why'd you keep it to

yourself?" He looked genuinely perplexed.

I told him how I hadn't wanted to let Mom and Dad down, how I thought I should focus on the acting role. "Plus, so many people – you included – had made it clear that I had no chance of making it as a music composer," I added.

Zeeshan looked down. "I'm sorry about that," he said. "I realized afterwards that I'd been so caught up in my own goals that I hadn't even thought about you. You helped us compose *Dil Se* for the OBAs and we celebrated without you. At the time, it didn't seem like a big deal but I can see how it hurt you. I should have supported you more."

The apology was heartfelt. I was touched. "I missed hanging out with you."

"Me too," he said. "I realized all of this when you weren't in the Noise Zone with us anymore. It wasn't as much fun. When Bolly Bop went viral, I was really happy for you."

"Thanks, Zee," I said, smiling. I hugged him.

"I know it doesn't matter that you're a girl. You should have the same opportunities to compose music for movies as I do. I spent a lot of time thinking about it recently," he went on. "I even wondered if I deserved the mentoring program... Maybe you should have been given it. At least you should have had a chance to go for it."

"*Awww*, you guys are too cute," smiled Joya.

I offered her a chocolate as Raktim bounded into the room.

"I can't believe you made that tune and kept it secret!" said Raktim, lifting me up in the air. He put me down and we did our special high-low, side-to-side fist bump.

"And you..." He gave Zeeshan a playful punch. "You'd worked out it was Simi all along and hadn't even told us!"

I looked at Zeeshan. "That's true," I smiled. "He actually kept my secret secret."

"I take it you're gonna come back to music now, right, Sim?" asked Joya.

"You're all being so kind but I won't change my mind just because of Bolly Bop. That was just luck – it doesn't mean I can do it again and again. I need to be realistic and also think about my mom and dad."

Zeeshan grabbed another chocolate and stood up. "Keep an open mind, Simi," he advised. "We all should. We don't know for sure how we're gonna feel next year or the year after that. Choose a range of options so you can change your mind."

"But right now, forget the future – let's think about tonight! Shall we go to the disco?" asked Raktim. "It's in the Dance Hall. We should celebrate!"

It was one thing we all agreed on and we made plans to meet up after dinner at 7pm. I felt a bit guilty for not calling my parents but figured one night of fun couldn't hurt and I'd call them in the morning.

Joya and I had fun getting dressed up. We blasted the music as loud as we could without getting told off by dorm parent, Jannat. Joya donned a pair of navy jeans with a sequin pattern down the side and paired it with a sparkly butterfly-print top. I wore my favorite jumpsuit. It was black, yes, but it had sheer puff sleeves with a polka dot design.

"Stop running!" yelled Miss Jannat as we scooted down the corridor. "And don't forget to put your laundry out by 10am tomorrow morning!"

Joya turned to give her a thumbs-up and we rushed excitedly to the hall.

Zeeshan and Raktim had beaten us to it. They called us over to the dance floor which looked like it would soon be overrun. Pop, rock and Bollywood rang out across the hall. The crowds were going crazy as the latest bhangra hits were played. The infectious sound of the Punjabi drums – known as dhol – was too much for most people to resist. We danced so hard.

Then, unexpectedly, I heard a beat that I knew better than most. Zeeshan, Joya and Raktim screamed in excitement as they recognized the tune and joined in with everyone else who was doing the dance moves. It was such a short melody, the DJ was asked to repeat it again and again and I was videoed countless times as people danced with me and then posted reels on their social media accounts.

Suddenly, the school disco felt like it was a gigantic party to celebrate me and my tune. I was so proud of what I had managed to achieve. The last few months had been stressful to say the least but would I even change a thing if I could go back in time? I didn't think so. The only thing I would ask for now was for Priya to be there to celebrate with me.

"I'm so thirsty!" I told Zeeshan once they'd moved on to another track. I dabbed my sweaty forehead with a tissue as we headed over to the drinks counter where a staff member poured us a lemonade and cola. We sipped our drinks as we giggled at Raktim and Joya doing some goofy moves.

"You know what?" I said to Zeeshan as a thought came to me. "I need to contact Mirza Choudhary this weekend, after I've spoken to my parents."

"Oh, why's that?" he asked, swigging his drink while surveying the dance floor.

"Well, he reposted the tune on his account. That's

how it caught on. It would never have gone viral had Mirza not posted it. I barely had any followers – now I have 15,000! I have to thank him."

"Yeah..."

I took another gulp of my lemonade. "But I don't know how he came across my account in the first place." I looked at Zeeshan, who looked back at me with a twinkle in his eye. I stared at him for a good few seconds before he threw back his head and laughed.

"I'm sorry, Simi," he giggled. "I thought you would have figured it out by now."

"You?" I put a hand to my mouth and then laughed. "*You* sent it to Mirza?"

I was in disbelief but of course it made sense. It was far more likely that Zeeshan had sent the song to him than that Mirza Choudhary, legendary music composer, had clicked on the account of a nobody on his own accord.

I probed further. "But how did you contact him?"

"Well, first I sent him the video via DM and asked if he could post it. Of course I didn't get a reply – I don't think he even saw my message. So I asked my mentor Parag Shah if he could do me a favor and send it. Mirza follows Parag so it was easier that way."

"Why did you do it though, Zee? Why go to all that

effort?"

"I thought it was really catchy..." He paused for a moment then smiled sweetly at me. "Plus, it was your birthday."

I felt a warm glow inside. Zeeshan *had* been thinking about me on my special day.

"We weren't really texting each other then so I thought it would be a nice surprise for you if one of your fave music composers posted your video on their account on your birthday."

I took a big gulp of air. All this time, I'd been thinking Zeeshan was selfish, only worried about his own ambitions and not supporting me, and yet he'd gone to all these lengths to get my melody out there. It would never have gone viral had it not been for him. I hugged him, not caring we were at a packed school disco.

My heart was full. Zeeshan's actions meant as much to me as the success of Bolly Bop itself.

*

I was getting ready to put the laundry outside the door for collection when I was interrupted by a phone call. This was the call I'd been expecting. I couldn't put it off any longer.

"Simi! Is it true?" asked Mom breathlessly. "You're the Melody Queen? That Bop Bollywood viral trend is your tune?"

That was funny, but I didn't laugh. I told myself I had to stay calm. I needed to make Mom realize I wasn't going to disappoint her by changing my career plans.

"Mom, I'm still going to focus on acting," I said. "The video was something I made and then Priya did the dance and we posted it on my thirteenth birthday because we could and then my friend Zeeshan found it and sent it to Mirza Choudhary."

"Take a breath!" said Mom.

"I didn't know it would go viral. Honestly, I didn't. It hasn't affected our movie, has it? We're still in it, aren't we?"

To my amazement, Mom laughed. "Of course we're still in it," she said. "Why wouldn't we be?"

She had a point. I guess I was just nervous. I didn't want to mess things up for her again.

"Are you mad at me, Mom?"

"No! Why are you saying these things?" she questioned. "I'm proud of you! I can't believe it was you. I'd heard the tune but I didn't know my daughter was behind it! We even did it in Lonavala," she reminded me. "My daughter is the Melody Queen!"

I was so relieved that she was laughing. I felt like I'd been worrying over nothing all along.

"Mirza Choudhary called us and said he wants to use it in one of his movies. He's asking for your permission," she told me.

My hands started shaking. The phone slipped and fell to the floor. I grabbed it again.

"Wh...what?"

Joya stared at me with a worried expression. I must have looked like a nervous wreck!

"Really?"

"Yes," Mom replied. "Really! How do you think we found out Melody Queen was you!"

"He knows?" I asked, shocked.

"Well, he didn't know when he posted the tune but a composer friend of his in the industry told him this morning. Parag...I forget his last name. Anyway, Parag is mentoring someone at your school who told him you were the Melody Queen and he passed on the information to Mirza."

Another warm glow came over me as I realized that Zeeshan had gone all out to help me achieve my goals.

"What a sequence of events!" Mom laughed out loud.

I was confused. "But...but I thought you hated me having anything to do with music, Mom?"

There was a small pause, before Mom explained: "I only ever discouraged you because I didn't want you to struggle like I did. I didn't want you to enter a profession where you have even less hope and fewer opportunities than I had," she went on. "I want you to succeed, not feel like a failure, like I do most of the time."

That got me. I had to sit down. The tears were pricking my eyes. I knew how much she had struggled.

"I'm proud to say you're far braver than I ever was. I'm proud you embrace who you are and make people accept you for what you are. You're an inspiration to me, Simi. I want to be more like you. I can start by learning to enjoy every decade of my life rather than always wishing I was in a different one."

Mom's words meant more to me than I could say. I'd always felt like I was failing her, that I could never do anything right. Maybe I wasn't perfect, but maybe that was okay. Maybe I could just be me.

Dad took the phone and, just as well, because the tears were starting to trickle down in earnest now. Joya brought over a box of tissues and I could see from her relieved expression that she had realized they were happy tears.

"My South Indian girl did it!" yelled Dad.

I laughed, hiccupping through the tears.

"And all those people who constantly told us we needed a son – well, they all now want a daughter like you," Dad said. "Even if you do nothing in the industry ever again, you've made a mark. I want you to always fight for what you want. I want you to always pursue your dreams," he said. "You've already made a far bigger impact than most men ever will. Maybe this is what the universe has planned for you."

Dad's comments touched my heart. I couldn't believe they were telling me I actually had a choice! Having the freedom to decide for myself meant so, so much – whichever choice I made in the end.

"Can I say yes to Mirza Choudhary?" Dad asked. "Take his offer before some other producers steal your tune – no money and no acknowledgement?"

"Yes!" I jumped up. "Why would I say no?"

I got off the phone and grabbed Joya. We spun around and around and around as I told her about my deal.

There was one other thing I had to do: I Facetimed Priya and told her all about it.

"Oh didi!" chuckled Priya. She was beaming from ear to ear. "I can't believe that the tune will be used in an actual movie!" She clapped her hands excitedly.

"It wouldn't have happened without you," I told her.

"No, I only did a silly dance," Priya said humbly. "The

dance isn't being used in the film – it's the music!"

"Yes, but without the so-called silly dance, the music would never ever have reached all those people. Thanks so much, Pri. I won't ever forget how we did this together. And I really, really want you to think about entering the next series of Dance Starz. You could be the next Bela!"

Priya, speechless, was obviously touched by my words. She cupped a hand over her mouth and giggled.

My aunt and uncle appeared on the screen and laughingly told me off for keeping this secret from them. I was so glad they seemed to be enjoying the whole experience. After chatting for a few minutes, I got ready to end the call and waved goodbye to Priya.

"Take care, Simi didi. I'm so glad you made it!" Priya said.

"No, sis," I replied. "*We* did."

TAKE TWENTY

The last day of the school year was always emotional, but this one was going to be even more so. I had to look my best. I combed through my wet hair and then scrunched some mousse in to create some curls.

"Here, Sim," said Joya. She passed me one of her clear lip glosses.

I smiled back at my reflection.

What a year it had been. So many ups and downs. But I had finally found myself.

Joya and I made our way to the Observatory where Zeeshan and Raktim were waiting for us.

"Your big moment!" said Zeeshan, lifting me off the ground.

"Zee!" I screamed playfully. "Put me down!"

"Now, now," came a male voice. It was Mr. Pereira.

"Be careful, children," Miss Takkar said as she strolled alongside him.

Zee let go and I landed on my feet. "No way! They're linking arms!" he exclaimed.

All the students around began whispering excitedly.

"She's wearing a ring!" I yelled out. "*Naaaaahhhhhh!*

They're engaged?"

"It's not a ring," stated Raktim. "It looks more like the Kohinoor diamond! Did you see the size of it?"

Frenzied chatter about the couple continued as we filed into the Observatory but died a sudden death as Mrs. Arora walked in, clapping her hands loudly for attention.

"This is a special treat for Grade 7s on the last day of the school year," she said. My breathing quickened. I was nervous.

"Since it's the last assembly of the year, we're going to begin with a special screening of a song from a movie that was released last week. This song got the Bollywood Academy quite a bit of attention this year!"

Zeeshan, sitting next to me, nudged me with his elbow. "Can you believe this?"

I shook my head. I really couldn't.

The clip began. The familiar melody of the Bolly Bop rolled out and happy tears were trying to force their way out of my eyes.

The Grade 7s screamed out, many of them standing up from their seats to mimic the perfect moves of Perfect Priya. Of course, Mirza Choudhary had added classical elements to the tune but he had retained the essence of my melody.

As the song ended, a single screen of the movie credits was shown. My eyes widened and a gasp escaped.

Music: Mirza Choudhary;
Bolly Bop song: Simi Prasad

The cheers were deafening. Raktim and Zeeshan hoisted me up, much to my embarrassment. It seemed like ages before they put me down again.

When I looked up, Mrs. Arora had taken a seat and Mr. Joshi was standing at the podium.

"I wanted to speak today because the huge achievement we are celebrating is a musical one. I would like to take credit for it but I can't," he said.

He turned to look at me.

"Simi, I owe you an apology."

All heads turned in my direction. I focused on his face, not blinking and barely allowing a breath to escape.

"Most of us are aware that in Bollywood movies, around 98% of composers from the past and present are men," he started. "Simi questioned why this was and I had no real answers to give her."

He paused, as if he was about to say something painful.

"She told me that she wanted to compose music for

movies and I told her not to do it. As a teacher who is meant to nurture our students and help them shine, this was obviously a pretty grave failure of judgement on my part." He dabbed his head with a handkerchief. "I was trying to stop her from entering a profession where she may face obstacles and closed doors. In doing that, I shattered her dreams and for that, I'm truly sorry."

I nodded, humbled by his words.

"I don't know if this is a result of Simi's success with Bolly Bop but we have more girls taking up music next year than ever before. Above all, I'm so glad that Simi has decided to major in music from Grade 8."

Joya and Raktim lead the cheers that went up while Zeeshan put an arm around me.

"I am so happy that Simi proved me wrong," confessed Mr. Joshi. "If you have the talent, the message should be to never give up. Simi, please, never give up."

I found it really difficult to sit still for the rest of the assembly. My mind was bursting with excitement. I wanted to run around Kohinoor Island screaming with joy.

"We have one more announcement for you," said Mrs. Arora. "Maybe some of you have noticed something rather sparkly on Miss Takkar's hand?"

I screamed. "Told you!" I said to Zeeshan as we both

stood up and yelled "Congratulations!"

Miss Takkar and Mr. Pereira stood up, appreciating the cheers. She held up her hand to show off her rock while Mr. Joshi took some photos of the pair.

"No doubt headline news for our summer newsletter," said Zeeshan as we filed out.

"Can you believe it, guys?" I said, looking at my bandmates. "We've actually managed to work with big names like Mirza Choudhary and Parag Shah this year."

"It's been crazy, dost!" said Raktim.

"Not as crazy as this!" said Zeeshan. He held up his phone and played a video clip: it was DJ Dan on stage at a show. I let out a small scream when I realized he was playing Bolly Bop and doing the moves at the same time.

"This tune was composed by the daughter of my childhood hero, Shyam Prasad," DJ Dan told his audience. "Her name's Simi. Look her up. Follow her. She's the one and only *Melody Queeeeeeeen!*"

IT'S A WRAP

music studio
NOISE
ZONE

perfect priya
BOLLY BOP
Joya
B-TUNES
RakTim
Mirza Choudhury
Recycled
#WhoisMelodyQueen?
BOMBAY MIX
authentic + delicious!
The BEST

Acknowledgements

Firstly, thanks to my fabulous publisher, Lantana, for all the support and enthusiasm for the Bollywood Academy series. Founder Alice Curry shared my vision for this series from day one, making it so much easier and more fun to write these books.

Hugs to Sinéad Gosai and Kristel Buckley for their tireless effort in organizing the *Starlet Rivals* launch and for managing press, PR and author events. Thanks also to the lovely Katrina Gutierrez for all the work behind the scenes in a different time zone.

I'm very grateful to Krystle Appiah and Caroline Carpenter for all their help and suggestions while editing *Melody Queen*. Their guidance allowed me to make this book the best it could be.

Jen Khatun's illustrations are, again, pure magic. I could stare at all the lovely detail for hours!

A special mention goes to Kuljit Bhamra MBE – composer, record producer and musician – for his invaluable input and advice about everything to do with music.

Thank you to my daughter Tara for her full-on enthusiasm for the Bollywood Academy's social media accounts. I could never keep those TikTok dances and reels coming without her!

A big kiss to my eldest, Roma, for her complete faith in this project and all the positive vibes she brings.

To Jas and Arjun – I fully appreciate the encouragement and support you both give and for always having the patience to listen to me chattering incessantly about my books.

Love to my mom, dad, mother-in-law and the Bhandal Familia for everything they do for me.

Finally, thanks to everyone who has bought a copy of *Starlet Rivals* or *Melody Queen*, reviewed the books, booked me for an author visit, liked or shared my social media posts or showed their love and support in other ways. You give me the inspiration to keep on writing.

Puneet

xoxo

About the author

Puneet Bhandal grew up in West London as a huge fan of Bollywood cinema but struggled to find anything to read that would connect her to her country of origin.

Her first writing job was as a Bollywood film journalist for a London-based newspaper. As the Entertainments Editor of Eastern Eye, Puneet enjoyed behind-the-scenes action on Bollywood film sets. The Bollywood Academy was born from her observations of real-life Bollywood personalities.

Challenging gender norms is no easy task, especially in industries where traditions and stereotypes are strong.

By bringing a character like Simi to life through *Melody Queen*, she hopes that we will have more female role models in traditionally male occupations, and that men and boys like Mr. Joshi and Zeeshan will be there to support them!

Puneet has spent more than twenty years working as a journalist and editor for a range of newspapers, books and magazines. She has also founded her own occasionwear boutique, with her dresses featured in *Vogue*, *Hello!* and other fashion magazines. "Miss England 2019" chose to wear one of her dresses at the competition finals. One of her favorite jobs is running Bollywood-themed creative writing workshops for schools – complete with a Bollywood dance demonstration!

About the cover artist

Jen Khatun is a children's book illustrator of Bangladeshi/Indian heritage who grew up loving all the costumes, dance sequences, and songs from the countless Indian Bollywood movies she watched as a child. Jen lives and draws by the coast of East Sussex.

The Bollywood Academy Series
by Puneet Bhandal

Set in Mumbai, India, this dazzling school series, packed with endearing characters, true-to-life relationships and authentic cultural details, charts the fortunes of students at the city's most prestigious stage school. Home to future film stars and movie producers, the Bollywood Academy sets the stage for the students to make friends, break friends, plot revenge and most importantly dream big as they prepare for life on — or off — the silver screen. Full of stylish outfits, fabulous film shoots, and one too many brushes with the paparazzi, this series is as glamorous as its star-studded cast.

The *Intasimi Warriors* Series
by Shiko Nguru

Set in modern-day Nairobi, Kenya, this thrilling series follows four young friends as they learn to wield their new-found powers as the descendants of the Intasimi: an ancient bloodline of legendary East African warriors. Follow Mwikali, Odwar, Soni and Xirsi as they race against time to learn how to channel their ancestors' powers while pitting themselves against a terrifying array of malign forces that are intent on using dark magic to destroy everything the friends hold dear. Inspired by the author's Kenyan heritage, this fast-paced, action-packed series is bursting with East African mythology and gripping to the very end.

In case you missed it...

An Extract from Starlet Rivals

Book 1 of The Bollywood Academy Series

TAKE ONE

I was transfixed. Fully focused on the TV screen. There was pin-drop silence, which was amazing for a room crammed so full of people that there was barely space to move.

"And the winner is..."

"*Eeeeeeeeekkkkk...*" I squeezed the arm of my bestie, Priyanka. A little too hard, apparently.

"Ouch!"

"Sorry, Pri!" I said. "I'm just so nervous. It's taking forever!"

"*Shhh!*" said Auntie Brinda from the other end of the sofa.

I was about to answer back but Raman Sood, the TV show host, spoke before I could. "*...Chintu!* Congratulations, Chintu – you're through to the finals!"

The room erupted. There was screaming, shouting, jumping, cheering.

"He's done it!" I yelled, leaping off the sofa. "Oh wow! He's actually done it!"

Chintu had won. The "slum kid" who defied the odds to win five heats of Dance Starz – the biggest TV talent show in India – had scored a place in the final.

Everyone was buzzing and talking over each other.

"I told you he would do it!" proclaimed Daadi, my grandma. She looked so proud, you'd be forgiven for thinking that Chintu was her own grandson.

"Ma, you always say that – no matter who wins!" my dad shot back.

I grabbed a corner of Priyanka's T-shirt, tugging her towards the door. "Let's go to my room," I whispered, edging past Auntie Poonam who had started waving her arms around in an impression of Chintu's winning dance.

"What are we gonna do when the show's over?" Priyanka asked as she planted herself on my bed. She lifted my new eyeshadow palette off my dresser and got to work on my eyelids. She was great at makeup, while I was terrible, and she always insisted on giving me a makeover when she came to visit. "I love Dance Starz so much. Chintu was just...amazing! I mean, how is he so flexible? Those back flips!"

Priyanka wasn't the only one who had been swept up in the talent show's craze. Even though this was the first season, it seemed that there wasn't a single family in India that wasn't glued to their screens on Friday nights.

I had seen every episode. Sometimes, when I was in

my room alone, I would pretend I was on the show. I'd do the whole routine, imagining someone was introducing me, and then I'd dance and fantasize that the crowd was going wild for my performance.

Priyanka continued to sweep the shimmery green eyeshadow across my lids, taking a step back to check her work.

"You know, you should have entered, Bela," she said. "You could have been on your way to fame and riches."

I opened my eyes wide.

"Keep them shut!" she scolded.

"Are you crazy?" I asked. "Me? Enter Dance Starz? I mean, yes, I'm classically trained, but these TV shows want that modern, stunt kind of dancing. I can't even do a single back flip!"

Priyanka laughed. "It's a dance show, not a circus!" She snapped the little box of shimmer shut. "You're a great dancer, Bela. I don't know anyone as good as you."

I smiled. She always championed me, even though I was nowhere near as good as she thought I was. Priyanka was the definition of BFF.

Continued in
Starlet Rivals (2022)